Leaving is My Colour

Leaving is My Colour

Amy Burns

**FREIGHT
BOOKS**

First published 2017

Freight Books
49–53 Virginia Street
Glasgow, G1 1TS
www.freightbooks.co.uk

ISBN 978-1-911332-23-7
eISBN 978-1-911332-24-4

Typeset by Freight in Plantin
Printed and bound by Bell and Bain, Glasgow

the publisher acknowledges investment from
Creative Scotland toward the publication of this book

Amy Burns was born in Birmingham, Alabama in 1969. She earned two BAs in English and Philosophy from the University of Alabama at Birmingham and a PhD from the University of Glasgow. She is Managing Editor of Mulberry Fork Review and has served as editor for anthologies of short prose.

Rock bottom is as rock bottom does.

I knew I was in love with Jack the summer he drowned.

The only person that noticed him drowning was an off-duty paramedic. She screamed, 'Call 911,' then jumped into the water. When she reappeared she had Jack from behind, Heimliching him furiously.

We knew he was all right when he screamed for her to stop.

I was never sure whether it was the idea of losing Jack forever that urged me over that line of friendly discretion or if it was the idea of another woman thrashing about with him in the water.

I discussed it with my best friend Phillip who also happened to be Jack's younger brother.

His take on the situation was simple. He said, 'You're the most insecure egomaniac I know.'

My father once told me: Things aren't always what they seem. I wouldn't disagree. In fact, I think things are rarely what they seem (especially when they are seemly). As for myself, I've only been certain of one thing in my entire life: loving Jack. I am still certain. I've just changed my mind.

My opinion of love is spurious. Elements just beyond the peripheral are at work. It's like trying to determine the correlation between a spike in violent crime and a spike in ice cream sales. The relationship seems real until you take into account a third factor acting on each: temperature.

Jack said our relationship failed because I refused to let go of a preconceived notion about love. I think it had more to do with him marrying somebody else.

★ ★ ★

People have said that I am an acquired taste. A little of me goes a long way.

Halloween, 1969. I was born. My three-year-old sister wasn't happy. Julie had asked for a puppy and they brought me home instead. She was put on infant homicide watch after my parents caught her trying to squirt dishwashing detergent up my nose. Our relationship hasn't improved.

My parents didn't plan to have a second child. Mother went off the idea of making babies after she saw what my sister did to her waistline. Mother referred to me as an accident. My father described me as a surprise.

Since I can't claim responsibility one way or the other for my birth, I've traced most of my problems back to my first real mistake.

There *was* an incident when I was four-years-old. I dropped my bottle from the car window and stuck my head out to look for it. Mother rolled up the window and didn't unroll it until sometime after I'd lost consciousness. Because that's my first memory, I don't think it should count. Having no other references from which to judge Mother's parental aptitude, and thus gauge the likelihood that she would roll my neck up in a window, lessens my accountability. My first *real* mistake happened when I was five. I ran away from home on my Hasbro Inchworm, travelling at speeds approaching one hundred and twenty feet per hour. The mistake? I didn't keep going.

★ ★ ★

I never thought I'd be the kind of person who could say things like, 'Yes, I've spent a little time in jail', or, 'If you count second cousins then, yeah, I've had sex with a relative'. I also never thought I'd be married and divorced enough times for it to be financially sensible to invest in a courthouse parking permit. But, there you go.

I didn't set out to become a serial monogamist. Decisions

seemed to make themselves although it's more accurate to say that I let go of the reins (if indeed I ever had hold of them) and things just happened. I married and divorced four times, toyed with addiction, lost my job and resurrected an interest in collecting state spoons.

I also had three major car accidents in the span of seven weeks. My insurance company wasn't pleased. One of those accidents involved my unmanned vehicle and a house.

When I realized the car was moving, I tried to get back inside but the door was locked and, with no time to remedy that, I did what I thought was the most logical thing: I jumped behind the car, planted my feet and tried to stop its backward progress. I've never been any good at math but, as I leveraged my weight against the ton and a half of steel and moulded plastic, I had time to work out a few simple equations. None of them were in my favour. I stepped out of the way.

When the policeman arrived, I said, 'I can't tell you how stupid I feel.'

He said, 'Try.'

'I considered getting in the car and faking a heart attack.'

'That plan has flaws.'

'Yeah, well, I couldn't get the door open for starters.'

He was pleasant enough after I passed the breathalyser. His expression said it all: amused condescension. He had me pegged. If I wasn't legally drunk, he assumed I must be one of those people that wander around perpetually flabbergasted by life.

I wouldn't say he was wrong. The officer managed to pry open the passenger side door and told me, 'Try to drive it home, a tow truck will be a waste of money.'

It made for an unfortunate scene what with the trunk horseshoed into the back seat, two flat tyres slapping against the pavement and sparks flying from the remains of a mailbox wedged underneath.

Sure, divorce is a bastard but hanging around the courthouse wasn't all bad.

The building itself was impressive. It was built in 1891 by a wealthy Prussian named Alfred Minuit. Minuit wasn't an architect but what he lacked in training, he made up for in palatial overstatement.

One might assume that Minuit's penchant for French Baroque and Romanesque Revival fit right in given the south's antebellum tendencies but people in Alabama were sceptical. That scepticism became full-blown hostility when Minuit imported in his own workers.

There has been some form of bloodshed every year since the courthouse opened. The most significant was when Walter Little dressed as a mailman and delivered a pipe bomb to Judge Benjamin Tolbert.

Judge Tolbert had dropped the gavel on Little's son who was serving eighteen months, minus good behaviour, for the rape of a *coloured girl* and, in an unrelated trial, was sentenced to a consecutive term of five years for tax evasion. Walter Little could not be consoled nor could he be convinced that his son wasn't the victim of a gross miscarriage of justice.

The bomb killed Judge Tolbert and his secretary. I learned this from reading a brochure which was printed by the Historical Society.

Courthouse security was tightened. Bags were checked by hand and weapons were banned. Any item construed as a potential threat was confiscated. Gone were the days you could bring your gun, knife, or axe (yes, axe). But it was a subjective process and visitors were forced to part with such things as curling irons, fingernail clippers, jars of jam and wooden rulers. Authorities eventually installed a metal detector that looked like something from a low-budget, science fiction film. It hummed.

The guards had to physically search me because I kept setting off the alarm. The culprit was a metal spoon I used to secure my hair in a twist. I wore it like that a lot during the divorce decade. I also boycotted make-up, undergarments and the practice of shaving smooth my underarms and legs. Showers fell by the wayside as well, not because I didn't want to be clean but rather, some undeterminable childhood fear resurfaced and I decided that I *really* didn't like getting my shoulders wet.

I landed somewhere on the spectrum between dishevelled and ripe hobo. I was still somewhat acceptable for work but rough-and-tumbled never came together for me as a fashion statement. There was no mistaking me for cool. Strangers felt comfortable asking me if I had a safe place to sleep at night and reminding me that Jesus looks after all his sheep, even those that have lost their way.

My self-esteem was like a bruised peach. Going out in public brought on panic attacks that made my blood run thick and hot, while my skin remained perfectly cool and crocodilian. And that was just on a trip to the grocery store. Imagine what it was like when I went to the courthouse where I not only was legally acknowledging the abject failure of yet another relationship but also faced the very real possibility of running into Jack. He was an attorney in Birmingham and, although Phillip had assured me that Jack avoided family law like a, 'a bag of itchy assholes', I couldn't help but be on constant look-out. I waited for the moment I'd hear his voice, half-questioning, half-astonished, 'Rachel is that you?'

Phillip suggested that's why I got divorced so many times, just so I could force a seemingly chance encounter. He said, 'I bet you walk around with a soundtrack playing in your head. Envisioning Jack scooping you up from the tobacco-splattered floor, a chapped, threadbare shadow of your old self.'

I told him to stop being so dramatic. 'They don't allow people to spit tobacco on the courthouse floor anymore.'

But of course I'd be lying if I said that I didn't spend time fantasizing about meeting Jack as I waited at the courthouse, watching people there to renew their driver's lisense or pay property tax or declare bankruptcy. And anxious though I was about seeing him, I admit, I even ventured down the halls pretending to be lost while really just looking for him. I'd come early and stay late, wandering the marble corridors which were lined with portraits of governors and judges. I recognized the more recent paintings. They were done by a local artist named Jim Yancy. I knew Jim. He lived with us for a while.

Jim was a half a bubble off plumb. He had a tendency to lend these officious, serious-minded men a rather demented, comedic look. I assumed they were all thinly veiled self-portraits.

During our first meeting, he sprawled himself on a yoga mat, in an impressive Hanumanasana, the monkey pose, an advanced position in hatha yoga, while explaining the extrapolative art of reading eviscerated chicken innards.

'Don't use roosters,' Jim said. 'They're unreliable, shiftless and have their own agendas.'

Many of Jim's upper-crust friends tolerated his eccentricities, thinking it made them chic by association. They tolerated him because he was a Democrat-voting artist who had the nerve to go unbathed and still expect the best table in a restaurant. They attributed his odd behaviour to his highly-tuned cultural sensibilities. I think Jim's odd behaviour had more to do with conspicuous consumption of pornography and PCP.

★ ★ ★

One of the judges that Jim captured on canvas, Judge Malcolm Hollister, presided over all four of my divorce proceedings and wasn't shy about expressing his disapproval.

As my fourth divorce drew to a close, Hollister said, among other things, 'Connor Lloyd McMann and Rachel Elizabeth

Bennett McMann, will you both please stand and approach the bench. One of you, at least, knows the path very well.

'Your divorce is granted by leave of this court on the grounds of those handy *irreconcilable differences*. And I have to ask, Rachel Elizabeth Bennett McMann, which of these words from your wedding vows do you have trouble understanding: love; honour; sickness and health; God; and until death do us part? They seem fairly straightforward to me, and yet here you are, standing before me for the fourth time seeking to revoke your sacred vows.

'Young woman, you are a stain on the fabric of God-fearing Christians. You have no respect for the holy union between man and woman. I pray that the Lord delivers you from the hands of the Devil and shows you the righteous path.'

I said, 'Thank you.'

Hollister added, 'Mister McMann… you have the sympathy of the court.'

Hollister was involved in a Supreme Court case, fighting for the right to display the Ten Commandments in his courtroom. He said these were rules from which everybody could benefit, 'Especially hedonistic, non-believing trash.' If Hollister had had his way with me, I'd wear only frocks and would never dance, vote or masturbate (you can buy a gun in Alabama but not a sex toy). I would have spent my days obeying my husband, making babies and, if the rumours concerning Hollister's Pentecostal practices were true, taking up serpents.

In the end, Judge Hollister was forced into early retirement. During an arraignment he called the defendant a 'white nigger'. His only public statement on the matter was, 'Right is right, no matter how you say it.'

I never was sure who led the protest to depose Judge Hollister – the blacks or the whites. They both seemed equally offended by the miscegenation of terms.

★ ★ ★

I did make one acquaintance during the 'I'm in the middle of a divorce' decade: Bailiff Eddie Walker.

Our first conversation began in the snack bar after I chipped a tooth on a frozen jellybean. Eddie was sitting at the table next to me.

He asked, 'Are you all right?'

I had my whole fist virtually in my mouth trying to assess the damage.

'I just chipped the hell out of my tooth.'

'I thought you might be having a seizure.' He handed me a napkin.

'I should devote the rest of my life to raising public awareness as regards hazardous frozen yoghurt toppings.'

'You'll need a slogan and a celebrity sponsor.'

'What colour lapel ribbons should I use to market the campaign? All the good ones are taken.'

Eddie finished eating a junkyard slaw dog while I explained the ways in which a divorce is worse than a root canal. He tried to be sympathetic, but he wasn't buying it. Eddie was a self-professed family man: one daughter, one son and one chocolate-coloured Labrador Retriever. He had been married to the same woman for eleven years and claimed not only to love her but to like her.

When I asked how they met, he was reluctant to say. But he eventually mentioned something about the internet and a singles chat room. The courtship consisted of instant messaging and emails. A cyber ballet ensued: 'You show me your jpeg, and I'll show you mine'. After a few months of virtual dating, they shared the expense of a cruise to Bridgetown, Barbados. They ate a bad batch of curried goat and were glad to leave the West Indies, raring to get back home to the United States where you get ice in drinks and Coke 'tastes right'. The suffering brought them together.

After we got to know each other better, Eddie asked, 'Why do you keep putting yourself through this?'

I said, 'Everybody needs a hobby.'

'Take up knitting.'

'How do you think I met my last husband? Knit. Knit. Purl.'

He looked around and asked, 'Is he here yet?'

'That's him.'

'Geez, you can pick 'em. This one doesn't look like he could screw his way out of a wet paper bag.'

'Why do you think he brought *three* attorneys?'

There was an awkward silence, and I said, 'I better find a seat, looks like it's going to be standing room only today.'

'Hey, wait a minute. Take these.' Eddie gave me two tickets to an open air concert at the municipal park.

For the briefest moment I wondered, is he interested in me? The rush of curiosity came out in an exaggerated, 'How thoughtful.'

'Not really. It's free. The city's on a big public relations kick. My boss told me to hand them out to anybody who'd take them.'

★ ★ ★

I never did see Jack at the courthouse.

All that worrying, whether or not my hair was washed or my shirt was egg-splattered or if I smelled like a fairground, for nothing. Well, I won't say it was for nothing but I was worried about those things for the wrong reasons. I suppose it was like taking a fistful of all the wrong vitamins.

I did see Jack's car in the parking lot one day. My lawyer had asked me to meet him because my then soon-to-be ex-husband was holding me in contempt of court for shouting at him over some mail and a plastic garden gnome.

I knew it was Jack's car because Phillip told me, 'He's gone out and bought a red, two-seater sports car for a family of four. I mean, his wife drives a minivan for Christ's sake. You're not gonna believe what he put on his vanity plate.'

'Shut your mouth. He has not got a vanity license plate.'

'Oh but he does and it reads: *JACKIN*.'

And sure enough, it did.

I moved my car to a more desirable spot; one better suited to watching than being seen.

Owning fast, fine cars had been a passion of Jack's for as long as I could remember. When we were kids he used to cut out pictures of cars, glue them to poster boards, and hang them from his bedroom ceiling. I felt genuine excitement that he had finally got a toy for himself and yet there was a tightening in my chest because the circumstances under which his dream had been delayed were severe and involved me.

He had tried to be happy for me when I turned sixteen and my father bought me a new 300ZX. It was a sweet ride, no mistake. And, in truth, Jack drove it more than I did. I loved that he loved it. Sometimes, with the radio blaring, the windows down, and the asphalt gripping the tread at over a hundred miles an hour, I thought he could go fast enough to forget that the car was really mine.

But all of that was before Jack and me and his old springer spaniel, Winston, went for a drive to the lake one Sunday afternoon during my junior year of high school and Jack decided to show a guy who was riding a Harley Davidson along I65 just how fast my car was.

When it all went wrong and we started spinning great circles, first on the pavement and then into the median, I tried to hold onto Winston but I couldn't make my arms work against the centripetal force and when the car started to flip, I remember that first lick as the back of my head broke a window but after that, I don't remember anything for many days.

Winston died.

We should have.

Jack had a hard time with what he'd done because it was excruciating for both of us and heartbreaking for that precious dog that looked to us for over a decade for love and treats and protection. He cried and told me later, 'I'll kill myself if you tell me to. I can't stand to live knowing I'm this weak and stupid.'

I was very young then. All I knew to do was hold him and tell him that I loved him and I asked him, 'Will you please just give me your pain? Give it to me and I'll hold on to it. And we'll both be all right.'

As I sat there looking at Jack's car that afternoon in the courthouse parking lot, my heart filled up with something heavier than blood. I wanted to take it out of my chest, wring it out and use it to wipe the sweat and tears from my face. I felt ashamed and sorry that he'd picked such an awful vanity plate for his beautiful, special thing. And most of all I wanted to think that the tag didn't represent him. I didn't want that to be his sense of humour.

I thought of Winston and how we all used to play in the yard. I thought of those long, suspended split seconds with my mouth wide and my eyes wide and my fingers gripping trying to claw his fur into my palms, trying to pull him to safety.

But me, I'm no hero.

I looked back to his car and took the spoon from my hair and let it fall down my shoulders. I mouthed, 'Where are you?'

I thought of all the stages of our lives that we've shared and how Jack and I have loved each other in many different ways.

First as babies: I've run naked through the sprinklers with you and didn't even notice that strange thing between your legs.

Second as kids: You're almost better than my big wheel.

Third as pre-teens: I don't mind being seen with you even though your arms are far too long for your body and you have something leafy and green stuck in your braces.

Fourth as teens: I don't know what you're doing but don't stop. Sex is the best thing since sliced bread.

Fifth as adults: You know all my dirty little secrets and have seen me at my worst. Why are you still around? I will be forever.

But Jack wasn't around forever. He married another woman. When it came down to telling his Jewish mother and father that he wanted to marry me, he wouldn't do it.

He told me this not long after I graduated from university, not long after he graduated from law school, and not long before he married a good Jewish girl named Joanie Hefetz.

He said, 'Rachel, you know I love you. Don't throw our life away.'

'I can't understand the words coming out of your mouth. Explain to me how I am throwing our life away?'

'Nothing has to change. Don't leave me. I don't want to lose you because of this. Everything can stay exactly the same. We just won't live together anymore.'

'So, let me get this straight. You want somewhere nice to hang your mezuzah and raise good Jewish babies but you still want to come around here and fuck me? What would the Rabbi say about that?'

'Please, don't do this to us.'

I said, 'It's already done.'

So, I waited in the courthouse parking lot all afternoon just to get a look at him but between the warmth of the car and the weight of my memories, I fell asleep. When I woke up, two hours were gone and so was Jack's little red car.

Marriage Counselling: A Scene.

Characters:
Randy Pickett (C): counsellor, bonsai enthusiast, avid cyclist.
Husband (H): then husband Connor, now ex-husband Connor.
Rachel (R): then wife Rachel, now ex-wife Rachel.

H: Sometimes she's just like a freaking goldfish.

C: No name calling, please.

R: I've been called worse.

C: Explain what you mean in a different way.

H: I don't know how to say it in a different way. A goldfish. No short-term memory. The plastic castle is a surprise every time.

R: Studies in fish behaviour have shown that to be a myth.

C: Rachel, please reserve comments for now. It's not your turn. Connor, please continue but I urge you to seek more concrete ways to describe what you're feeling. And remember, you can speak directly to her.

H: I just wish you'd remember some of the things we've discussed. I've told you over and over again the things that irritate me, and you just don't care.

R: So are you saying that I can't remember, or I don't care?

C: Rachel, please. Connor, could you give specific examples?

H: I hate it when she leaves make-up on the bathroom counter.

C: Speak directly to her, please.

H: I hate it when you leave make-up on the bathroom counter and when you leave make-up floating in the toilet.

We've talked about cleanliness in shared spaces like, I don't know, about a million times.

R: You know what I think is your biggest problem? Boredom. Anybody who contrives such an autocratic resentment over eyeliner shavings floating in the toilet has too much time on their hands.

H: Autocratic resentment? What are you talking about? You just don't see the big picture, do you? It's a sign of a larger problem. You don't care what I have to say about anything. You won't even take responsibility for the shavings.

R: I won't take responsibility for the *shavings*? What kind of needy, childhood fantasy are you trying to fulfil by trapping me in this room, paying sixty dollars for half an hour and demanding that I take full responsibility for the *shavings*?

C: Ok, let's stop for a moment and regroup. We're getting a bit distracted. Rachel, do you feel trapped right now?

R: Who wouldn't feel trapped right now? Sounds like my husband has been sieving eyeliner shavings out of the toilet and every time I try to breathe in this tiny-ass room I get molested by one of your little bonsai trees.

C: Let's focus and leave my little bonsai out of it for the moment.

H: It's obvious she doesn't want to work this out.

C: I wonder if what we are discovering is that each of you has slipped into defined, unhelpful roles. You have become the disciplinarian, the overbearing parent. You have become the mischievous child. But if you could relinquish those roles and come to see that there is actually much truth in the old adage, the couple that plays together stays together, then I think you could start over with a much healthier, happier outlook on your marriage.

R: It helps if you like the person you're playing with.

H: So now you're saying that you don't like me?

R: No, I didn't say that.

C: Well, you actually came pretty close to saying it,

Rachel.

R: This isn't horseshoes or hand grenades: close doesn't count.

Worry is my middle name.

As a kid, I worried.

I used to lie awake at night and wonder how far in advance I could hear an approaching nuclear warhead. Or, what it would be like to make eye contact with a suicide bomber seconds before detonation. Or, what I would do if someone broke into the house. My father had a .25 calibre Browning in his closet, and I wasn't afraid to *pretend* to use it.

I thought a lot about the state of the nation. I realize now that the nation gets along whether I worry or not. But I did feel sorry for Jimmy Carter. Southern boy made it to the White House, was labelled incompetent, attacked by a swamp rabbit while on a fishing trip, forced to watch his brother's Billy Beer advertisements and then, to top it off, shown up by jelly-bean-eating *Bedtime for Bonzo* Reagan. I like to think that Jimmy was too honourable to swap arms for hostages but look what it did for Reagan's career. It was no coincidence, twenty minutes after Reagan wrapped his inaugural speech, that Iran announced the release of the hostages.

It was the first time I can remember being old enough to follow politics and arrive at conclusions of my own. I was certainly old enough to understand the chilling concept of human fodder. I felt evil by proxy like, because I was American, I was responsible for ugliness done in the name of my country.

But, for me, guilt was a familiar costume. I felt bad because we had enough food and clean water. Indoor plumbing. Warm clothes. Orthodontists. Atari 2600. To make up for these comforts, I spent a great deal of time serving out self-imposed punishments.

One afternoon, I heard Mother calling me.

She came into the bedroom and asked, 'Have you seen your

sister?'

Julie said, 'Yes.'

'*Where* is your sister?'

'Under her bed.'

Silence.

Finally, Mother asked, 'What's she doing under the bed?'

Julie looked down at me. 'She's got her wrists tied with a sock and a bandana stuffed in her mouth. I assume she's pretending to be a hostage in... hold on a second.' Julie leaned down for dramatic effect. 'Where? I mean, I'm guessing Tehran. Nod if it's Tehran.'

I nodded.

She raised herself back into a comfortable seated position and answered Mother. 'She's pretending to be a hostage in Tehran.'

Mother left without saying anything else.

After one particularly desperate night, dreaming of death by earthquake, storms and steam explosions, Mother asked me why I looked so sour.

'I don't look sour.'

'Don't tell me how you look. I'm the one looking at you.'

'I had a bad night.'

'You're eleven years old, how can you have a bad night?'

Julie looked up from the Lifestyle section of The New York Times, a newspaper which always arrived at our house by mail two days late. 'She's upset about this whole Mount Saint Helens thing.'

'What Mount Saint Helens thing?'

I said, 'It erupted is what.'

Mother looked confused for a moment. 'I didn't think volcanos still did that.'

Julie gave a fawn-like smile in Mother's direction. 'Don't trouble yourself, Mother. We're not talking Pompeii.'

I put my head in my hands. 'I can't stop thinking about all those people dead and all those animals burned up.'

'It doesn't do any good to obsess over things like that. Anyway, you shouldn't use the misfortune of others as an excuse to be in a bad mood.'

It came out before I could think better. 'What's your excuse then?'

Julie choked on her chocolate milk.

'Don't you *dare* speak to me like that! I'm your mother. You have no idea what I go through.' She left the room and just before she slammed her bedroom door she screamed, 'And nobody likes a smart-ass.'

Julie tried to drive home the point. 'She's right. Nobody likes a smart-ass'

'Shut up, Julie.'

That particular time Mother refused to speak to me for six days. She's a professional when it comes to the silent treatment and I still don't know which is worse, when you have her attention or when you don't.

★ ★ ★

I tried various things as a child to both comfort and control myself. There was self-imposed discipline, tearing paper, and compulsive list making. But nothing made me feel better than being with my two best friends, Phillip and Jack Cohen.

They lived three doors down and were the only kids in the neighbourhood who would play with us.

They were Jews. They still are.

Rough estimate: at the time, less than 1% of the population in Birmingham, Alabama was Jewish. This put Phillip and Jack on the top five most-discriminated-against list which also included *blacks*, *women*, *gays* and *creationists*. *Vegetarians* almost made the list. However, at the time, general Southern opinion leaned more toward open ridicule than unabashed hatred.

For brothers less than a year apart, Phillip and Jack couldn't have been more different. Phillip was blonde, short and stout.

Jack was dark-haired, tall and slim.

Jack's looks had afforded him a confidence that Phillip didn't have even though, truth be told, Phillip was always smarter, funnier, and more compassionate than Jack. My relationship with Phillip was purely platonic but I think, in some ways, we knew each other more intimately than Jack and I did. Maybe that's because my relationship with Phillip could run to depths without the angst and filters that inevitably go along with growing up in love.

Of course, Jack's bravado masked a multitude of sins and insecurities but, by the time I found out about those, it just made me love him more. Jack knew how to carry himself; he knew what people wanted to hear and how to say it. He knew how to make you feel wanted. And for a long time, he wanted me.

But when we were just freewheeling kids, Jack was our hero and protector. That's probably where it all started with me. He protected me. He protected us.

One example, David Kimball, a pipefitter's son and the only kid on the block with a motorbike, was particularly cruel to Phillip. He said, 'You can't be a real Jew.'

Phillip said, 'I am so.'

'You sure don't look like one.'

'I do so.'

'No, you don't. None of the Jews in our history book look anything like you.'

Phillip said, 'How many Jews are in your history book?'

'I don't know, fool. I haven't counted them.'

'What's a Jew supposed to look like?'

David pointed to Jack and said, 'Like that. Jews are supposed to be dark, skinny bastards, not blonde, fat bastards.'

Jack said, 'That's enough, Kimball.'

'Your parents aren't Jews either if they let that pig in the house.'

Jack got off his bike and told Phillip, 'Hold this.' He took a few steps toward David. David took a few steps back.

Jack said, 'You scared, you Neanderthal?'

'That's a big word, Cohen. You must have a dictionary up your ass.'

'If your brow was any lower you'd trip over it. I'm not going to tell you again to leave my brother alone.'

'And what if I don't?'

'I'll take this dictionary out of my ass and beat you with it.'

Jack was skinny, but he'd held his own with David Kimball in more than one fight. David was dumb, but he wasn't stupid. He knew when to quit.

Every day there was a new drama. You'd have thought WWIII had started the afternoon Jack told them that Jesus was a Jew. Several of them shouted at the same time, 'He was not!'

'Sure he was.'

David Kimball said, 'How do you know Jesus was a Jew?'

'Lots of ways.'

'Name one!'

'He said so.'

'No, he didn't.'

'Yes, he did. In the Bible.'

David said, 'Maybe in your lying Jew Bible but not the *real* Bible.'

Julie was sitting on a brick retainer wall watching the melee unfold. She didn't play with us much because she was older and better. But sometimes she got bored enough to come outside and referee.

David was a big corn-fed American boy who, early on, was lucky (or unlucky) enough to find his father's stash of girly magazines. David freely admitted to doing vile things to himself with a sweat sock while looking at *Boobs & Toobs*. Because Julie was more 'developed', he assumed that she had something special up her skirt, and he always put on airs for her. He strutted over to her and said, 'Babe, why do you have anything to do with these devil lovers?'

Julie said, 'All religion is a load of voodoo.'

David looked stunned. He said, 'I had no idea you were a communist.'

Julie said, 'I'm not a communist. I'm an atheist, you moron.'

David's face turned red. 'You're going to hell!' And then he looked at me and Phillip and Jack, and he said, 'And you blaspheming fuckers are too!'

After that, the families who organized the neighbourhood watch (minus our families: Bennett and Cohen) met to discuss what should be done about the Communist/Satanists among them (i.e. the Bennetts and Cohens). They composed a letter chock-full of spelling errors and pseudo-legalese, posted a signed, notarized copy in each of our mailboxes and waited for us to test their faith.

The letter read as follows:

The <u>undersigned</u>, hereafter known as the <u>undersigned</u>, and the <u>underlined</u>, wish it to be known by affidavid that community objections have been raised with best regards to the nuisances porported to have been committed by various members of the Bennett and Cohen families. The <u>undersigned</u> and the <u>underlined</u> wish it to be known by said families that, post facto, porported nuisances will not be tolerated and that legal redress will be pursued and sought by the planetiffs from the plaintees should such happen again within their lifetimes. In particular, the <u>undersigned</u> (<u>underlined</u>) will seek judicial review through their lawyers in association with Church Elders concerning blasphemies (<u>various</u>) against Our Lord Jesus Christ who was not, in any case, and without prejudice, a Jew, nor did he associate with same except to overturn their tables in a <u>Temple of Ill Repute</u>. In particular, also, the <u>undersigned</u> (<u>underlined</u>) will submit further evidence to the State Legislature that Julie Bennett, in dilecto, publically blasphemed to the distress and detriment of miners by stating, (and we, the undersigned (<u>underlined</u>) quote thusly) <u>All religion is a load of voodoo</u>. This is not true.

Signed and Underlined...

Mother was devastated.

She wasn't interested in attending their potluck dinners or being invited to Super Bowl parties, but she couldn't stand to be ostracized. It fuelled many hours of deep thought, animated soliloquies and tearful pleas about what she'd done to deserve this.

Mother = martyr. Leisure pursuit taken to high art form.

★ ★ ★

It was more than just neighbourhood arguments that Jack tried to settle and whether or not he made it better or worse, I don't know, but at least he tried.

I was sitting in my room one afternoon, obsessively tearing sheets of paper from the phone book into tiny strips and folding even smaller yellow paper peonies out of those tiny strips, when all of a sudden I heard a thud on the wall. It happened again. Eventually one punch sent drywall spilling onto my bedspread. I could see the end of a hammer being dislodged from the hole and then Mother's face appeared on the other side.

She had decided to expand her bedroom which meant knocking down the wall separating us. When she realised that the job was too much for a single person with a handheld hammer (i.e. when she broke a fingernail) she called a professional builder to finish the job.

My bed was moved into Julie's room.

Julie perceived this as an act of open warfare.

Days passed during which she refused to speak to me unless in the presence of adults who might condemn such behaviour. Soon, the more substantial retaliations began. She told everybody at school that I still wet myself during the night. She put fire ants in my bed. The bites sent me into anaphylactic shock. Lucky that Minnie, our housekeeper, was smart enough to give me antihistamines and rush me to the emergency room. I was covered in hives and my lips looked like split sausage links.

I refused to speak to Julie when I got home. Once we were alone in our room she said, 'Don't be such a baby. It's not like you're dead or anything.'

It was Jack who put Julie in her place for hurting me.

When I was able to go out and play again, Jack and Phillip walked me down to a place in the park where Julie used to always go to read. It was a bench at the far corner of the pond where not many kids went because a lot of the old people took their walks purely for exercise over there and they had a tendency to stop and talk every time they made a circle around the pond. Julie didn't seem to mind talking to them, she was always so overly polite and fake. They all thought she was the most fabulous of girls.

We three found her there.

Now, it was always somewhat interesting with Julie and Jack because she always treated him with a respect that she didn't give most people. In retrospect, I suppose she might've had a little crush on him too. Her face lit up a bit when she saw him. She gave him proper smiles, not the grimaces I got. And when she saw us coming that day, even with me all marked up still, I don't think she expected him to be mad at her.

She looked over the top of her book which was covering most of her face. When we got close she said, 'Where are you off to?'

Jack said, 'Here.'

She gave him one of those smiles and put her book down.

He sat down at the picnic table while we stood behind him.

It didn't take long, what he said to her.

He said, 'Julie, you can act like a big girl all you want, be a bitch, act it out. Go ahead. Play whatever part you want. But

I know what you're really doing. And I know what the boys are saying about you at school. I know where you're going at night when you sneak out of your house. I know where Carolyn Hester's mother took you three months ago. I know inside you're just a mean little girl who is going to grow up to be a mean woman. And I don't care what you do, not really. Just as long as you don't do it to the three of us. And if you hurt Rachel again, I'll tell everybody where you went with Carolyn's mother.'

Julie's expression had gone blank. She was giving him no satisfaction. She just picked her book up and began to read. And he left it at that. They walked away faster than normal and I had to hurry to keep up.

I asked under my breath, 'Where did she go with Carolyn's mother?'

Jack said, 'I hope I don't ever have to tell you, Rachel.'

To ease the punishment for such an act of malice, and to get back at us for our show of solidarity, Julie told Mother that I had been doing naughty, sex things with Jack.

I was sent to see a psychologist.

I actually wasn't doing naughty sex things with anybody but after eleven visits with the psychologist I was curious to know what all the fuss was about.

The curiosity culminated in a game of show-and-tell behind the gardenia bush.

When Jack showed me his, he quickly covered it up and swore that it was bigger than that sometimes. If somebody had told me then that one day I'd marry anybody who'd sit still long enough, have not one but six drug dealers on speed dial, lose a job, lose a fortune and put my very existence in danger just because I couldn't see that knobby little tubercle, well... I'd have told them to fuck off, in the nicest way possible.

Therapy: A Family Affair.

Characters:
Dr Gabriel Holden (Dr): Psychiatrist
Rachel (R): Patient
Father (Dad): Guest
Mother (Mom): Guest
Julie (Sis): Guest

Dr: Come in. Come in. Make yourself comfortable. I thought we'd meet in here today so that there's a bit more room for everybody. Hello Rachel, how are you?

R: Fine.

Dr: Ok, if we can all just find a seat.

Mom: Louis, all the chairs in here have arms.

Dad: True.

Dr: Is there a problem?

Mom: No, there's no problem. I'll stand.

Dr: We might be quite some time. Surely you'd be more comfortable sitting.

Mom: I'm fine.

Dr: Let me put it another way. I think it might be slightly disruptive if you stand while the others are seated.

Dad: For God's sake Felicia, sit down.

Mom: All of these chairs have arms. I would prefer one without arms. Do you happen to have just a straightforward chair with no arms?

Dr: One second, let me see what I can do.

R: I knew this was a mistake.

Sis: Don't start. Everybody has preferences, if she doesn't want to sit in a chair with arms what's the big deal.

R: She's just being awkward and drawing attention to

herself.

Mom: I am not. It's for medical reasons. I can't sit in a chair with arms for medical reasons.

R: What kind of medical reasons?

Dr: Here we go. This is the best I could do.

Dad: Here let me help you with that.

Dr: Thanks. Rachel, would you help your father get that armchair out of the way, please. How's that? Better?

Mom: Yes, thank you. It's for medical reasons.

Dr: Ok, well, we want you to be comfortable.

Mom: It's medical reasons not comfort.

Dr: Ok. Phew. I've broken out into a bit of a sweat, please forgive me. Just one second and let me get a tissue. Goodness. Excuse me. I must be terribly out of shape.

R: I'm sorry.

Mom: Don't apologize for me.

Dr: Ok, let's begin. Shall we? My name is Gabriel and I am very pleased that you all took time from your busy schedules to be with us today. I think if we can talk as a group, it will be very helpful in Rachel's progression.

Mom: When you say your name is Gabriel what does that mean?

Dr: I'm not quite sure I understand the question.

Mom: Gabriel. When you say Gabriel does that mean that you aren't a doctor?

Dr: No ma'am. I'm a doctor. If you prefer you can call me Doctor Holden.

Sis: Holden, that reminds me of *The Catcher in the Rye*.

Dr: Exactly, that's it.

Sis: I'm an avid reader.

Dr: How interesting. We're getting a bit ahead of ourselves here. Rachel, would you do the honours of introducing everybody please?

R: This is my father, Louis Bennett.

Dr: Mister Bennett, would it be possible to finish your cell phone communication after the meeting?

Dad: Of course. I was just finishing an important text.

R: This is my mother, Felicia Bennett.

Dr: Nice to meet you Missus Bennett.

Mom: Likewise, I'm sure, Doctor Holden. But please do call me Felicia.

Dr: And, Rachel?

R: Yes?

Dr: Lastly we have?

R: Oh, my sister.

Sis: I'm Julie Bennett-Morgenstern, avid reader.

Dr: Yes, you mentioned that. Pleased to meet you. Mister Bennett, could I ask you to put your cell phone on vibrate or perhaps even turn it off?

Dad: Of course. No problem.

Dr: Well, as I said before I'm really happy that you could finally agree upon a time. From what I understand there have been several scheduling conflicts.

Mom: Yes, but Doctor Holden you must understand we would do anything to help Rachel on the road to recovery.

R: I'm not really on a road to recovery, Mother. It's just a therapy session.

Mom: Dear, if you're not then perhaps you should be.

Dr: In order to use our time to the fullest here's what I would like to do. If you don't mind I'll speak with each of you individually and then we can speak as a group again at the end of our session.

Sis: Actually, I do mind. Why can't we stay as a group?

Dr: Well, Julie… In my experience starting a family group therapy such as this, it is best to take a moment to get to know each member of the group prior to discussing particular topics *as* a group. I also think it serves to create a more comfortable atmosphere for the new members and promotes a sense of discretion which in the beginning, they may not feel comfortable sharing in front of others.

Sis: I think that's the point isn't it? I mean, I didn't come here today so that everybody could go behind my back and talk about me and then come back in here and smile to my face.

Mom: I have to say I don't see the point in that either.

Dr: Mister Bennett, we're all adults here. Please don't make me take the cell phone away from you. Please, sir. It's incredibly rude to continue after I've asked you to stop.

R: Dad, please put the phone away.

Dad: I am. I am. Sorry.

R: No, turn it all the way off.

Mom: Rachel, don't be so domineering. Your father is a busy man. He can't just stop the world from spinning because you've got a therapy appointment.

Dad: It's off darling. See look. It's off.

Mom: Really Louis, you don't have to do that.

Dr: Ok, if we can get back on track now, time's a wastin' as they say.

Mom: I have another appointment at three p.m. I don't think we'll be done in time if we split up. Let's have a vote. Who thinks we should meet as a group? Raise your hands.

Dr: I'm sorry Miss Bennett I'll have to revoke voting rights for now. Unfortunately, it isn't necessarily a democracy within these four walls.

Mom: Felicia, dear. Call me Felicia.

Sis: Actually, I've got an appointment this afternoon too.

Mom: What time?

Sis: Soon.

Mom: Could you give me a ride to Mountain Brook? I rode over with your father but he's got other plans for the afternoon I believe. Is that right Louis?

Dad: That's right Felicia.

R: Could we all just be quiet a moment and let Gabriel say what he needs to say.

Sis: Hand me my purse Mother. We need to go now if I have to drop you off.

Mom: Rachel, here before I go. Now, no offence Doctor Holden but, well... Rachel, dear, take this card. I think perhaps you should speak with my therapist. He's very nice and organized and he has a very commanding presence. It's experience, I think, Gabriel. Anyway, he's got Koi in his waiting room, they're terribly soothing to watch while you wait. That might be an idea for you Doctor Holden, Gabriel.

Dad: Would you like for me to stay?

R: No, it's ok.

Dad: Let me give my little girl a kiss then. Thank you Gabriel, take good care of her and good luck with the therapy sessions. Sounds like everything's going great.

R: Bye Dad.

Sis: Nice to meet you Gabriel, perhaps I could book a session?

Dr: I'm sorry. I'm not taking new patients right now.

R: I knew that would be a mistake.

Dr: No, it was useful.

R: I'm sorry.

Dr: No, I'm sorry.

The house that Rachel built.

Start thinking of an excuse now for the next time somebody offers you free tickets to an event sponsored by the city's public relations department. The tickets that Bailiff Eddie Walker gave me that day at the courthouse landed me at a concert where I met Daniel.

I didn't want to go alone so I took Emma, a girl I'd known since high school. She was the only person I could think to ask. Phillip lived in New York and as far as work acquaintances went, I preferred to keep them at work.

Emma and I founded our friendship on a mutual distaste for authority and a shared fear of public ridicule. I was singled out early in my school career. I never fit in. Emma was closer to acceptance, but she sustained a downturn in popularity when Bobby Tipton suffered a coincidental (but particularly nasty) outbreak of cold sores after they 'made out'.

Emma and I kept in touch. By that I mean she called me every now and then to tell me how things were going in her life. You could start a conversation with Emma by saying, 'I lost both arms in a wood chipper.' She would say, 'Oh my God! Let me know if you need anything. Listen, you're not going to believe who I slept with.'

The concert coincided with the three-week anniversary of Emma's latest failed affair. She didn't understand why he wanted to spend all major holidays with his wife. She said, 'Easter is lonely when you're somebody's mistress.' I'd have skipped the concert and opted for something more enjoyable like a bikini wax had I known that Emma was still in mourning.

To mark the occasion, she drank too much Jägermeister and spent most of the evening throwing up in a water installment commissioned by the Alabama Agricultural Society. Tapped into the granite base was an inscription which read: In honour of the sweet potato.

Daniel waited until Emma passed out before he came over to say hello. He pointed to her lying there in all her resplendent glory (mouth open, hair matted with vomit) and he asked, 'Is that yours?'

I said, 'Unfortunately so.'

'I hope you saved the receipt. I think it's broken.'

Without opening her eyes, Emma shouted, 'I can't find my shoe.'

Daniel said, 'She's wearing both shoes.'

'Cinderella syndrome. She's forever losing that damn glass slipper.'

He thought I was charming. I thought he was new.

* * *

Daniel worked as an accountant.

This was surprising because he had a sense of humour and at no time did he ask me if I filed my taxes using a short or long form. Also surprising was the fact that he seemed perplexed by basic math, was terrible with money and was always broke.

He claimed to be a direct descendant of Howard Hughes and said that he had been cheated out of his inheritance because of a botched DNA test. Daniel kept a picture of Hughes in his wallet and had a tattoo on his shoulder: Spruce Goose, the plane that flew but once. Appropriate.

We entertained each other with a shared pessimism.

We spent a great deal of time inebriated, exercising the shared mental capacity of an earthworm.

We travelled on my dime.

Home from work one afternoon, Daniel asked, 'Have you ever been to Halifax?'

I said, 'No, have you?'

'No, but my brother lives there.'

'I didn't know you have a brother.'

'There are lots of things you don't know about me.'

'Like what?'

'Oh no! That's a trick question.'

'How is that a trick question?'

'Women ask questions like that so that men will confess something and then they use it as artillery.'

He seemed pleased with himself as if he had successfully manoeuvred a preternatural obstacle course. I went back to reading the newspaper.

I said, 'Chile now has a woman president: Verónica Michelle Bachelet Jeria. Says here that she is a moderate socialist. I wonder what that means exactly, to be a moderate socialist? Hey, listen to this… she's a paediatrician/epidemiologist/single mother/agnostic with expertise in military strategy. She speaks five languages. I'd be happy if our president spoke one language fluently.'

'Are we going or not?'

'Going where?'

'Earth to Rachel! Halifax.'

'I guess.'

Daniel got a beer out of the refrigerator. He said, 'Forget it. If you're not going to be excited, we might as well not go.'

'What? Why do you do that? I *am* excited. I've never been more excited! Let's go!'

'Yeah, let's. It'll be fun.' He lifted the lid from a cooking pot and said, 'That smells good, what is it?'

'Soup.'

'I can see that. What kind?'

'Fish stew.'

'You didn't put squid in, did you? I hate squid.'

'You've mentioned that before.'

He opened the beer and leaned against the counter. He was staring at me.

I asked, 'What is it?'

'Nothing.'

'You're staring.'

'Jesus, can't I just look at you? I think you're pretty.' He stood there for a moment longer. He took a drink of beer. He picked something off the sole of his shoe. He refolded a dish towel and hung it on the oven door. Then he asked, 'You don't happen to have any cash, do you?'

'See! I knew you wanted something.'

'Oh, for fuck's sake. Forget it.'

'Why do you need cash?'

'My brother is getting married and I am the best man.'

'Is that the reason you're asking about Halifax?'

'I'm the best man. For God's sake, I think I should at least have the common courtesy to show up.'

'When is the wedding?'

'Tomorrow.'

★ ★ ★

I spent more time at Daniel's place than I did my own.

Before I knew it, I had closet space and a shelf in the medicine cabinet. Daniel owned two towels that looked like the rats had been sucking them. I bought new ones. He only had one set of sheets, stained. I bought new ones. The only coffee mug he had was shaped in the likeness of Wile E. Coyote. I bought new ones.

My hatred for Wile E. Coyote and The Road Runner is visceral. When I was a kid all it took to send me into screaming convulsions was to hear the theme to the show. This is one area in which Phillip and I were in total agreement. Jack could never understand what we were talking about and stood firmly on the side of Road Runner. It wasn't that I particularly *liked* the Coyote and it wasn't that I particularly *hated* the Road Runner. It was just that I absolutely could not tolerate knowing that the Coyote would try and try and try the whole cartoon to catch that Road Runner with no luck. And, as Phillip often pointed out, it wasn't that he failed but he often savagely mutilated himself in the process. It was the forever trying and failing.

I only went to my house occasionally to pick up mail, most of it from credit card companies threatening to turn me out to collection agencies.

Nothing in my house was where it should be. I had very little furniture. The mattress was still on the floor. I hadn't unpacked yet. Boxes were stacked high where the movers had left them.

I came over sometimes with the best of intentions. I spent time planning where I would put everything. I daydreamed about lining the kitchen cabinets and stocking the pantry. Painting the walls. Regrouting the bathroom. But as soon as I'd get started my attention span would shrink to that of a split pea and I'd give up.

I liked to call that lentil brain.

Daniel and I stopped by my house one evening to get a few books. I was going through a must-consume-vast-amounts-of-literature phase. Daniel wasn't much of a reader. He was more interested in watching sports highlights, playing Nintendo and mixing narcotics.

Daniel said, 'I don't see how you can stand to live out of cardboard boxes. Doesn't it bother you?'

I said, 'It would bother me a lot more if I had to live *in* one.'

'You know what I mean.'

'Of course I do. Can you imagine trying to get homeowners' insurance?'

'I'm serious. Wouldn't it make you feel better to unpack? Have a little more stable environment?'

I said, 'I'll get around to it.'

'How about now?'

I turned to face him, angry at his assumption that I gave a damn what he thought about my housekeeping. He was down on one knee. He held up a ring.

'Will you marry me?'

I feigned excitement, said yes, waited for a couple of months and deserted him as he slept in a hotel room in Salt Lake City. He snored while I pinned a note to his white, terry cloth robe. The note read: *Marriage shouldn't be a coward's playground. I'm doing you a favour.*

He must have agreed because I never heard from him again. I can only assume he still thanks me.

I had somewhat less to thank Daniel for, or so I mused as I stood in line at the Free Clinic waiting to get my Frequent Flyer card punched. I asked the nurse, 'Will I be able to get rid of this?'

She said, 'Nothing to worry about, love, just your everyday, garden variety STD.'

I made a mental note never to have a tossed salad at her house.

Most things I do, I don't want to.

Mother decided that I should be a Girl Scout.

I told her that I had no interest in being a Girl Scout.

She said, 'We all have to do things we don't want to.'

There it was. She hit me right between the eyes with the most annoying cliché in the history of man.

I don't understand why people feel the need to state the blindingly obvious.

It's self-evident and doesn't bear repeating. Julie (and Descartes) said that everything is self-evident. I don't know if I'd go *that* far.

Mother refused to give me a ride home from school on the given afternoon. I was left to join the ranks. Julie saluted me as they drove away.

The troop leader, Mrs McGuiness, opened a second-storey window and said, 'Hurry up and get your uniform on, Miss Bennett. We're about to leave for a glorious expedition!'

I was paralysed for a moment, trying to shake the horrific image of what breakfast must have been like at her house. I bet they went so far as to have animated conversations about their hopes and dreams. She probably insisted that her children set goals and stick to them. I guessed her family did things like play board games together and bob for apples at Halloween. When I finally settled on the startling image of her in a pastel nursery, running around screaming *duck, duck, goose*, I ran inside to get ready.

By the time I was dressed the other girls were out front and ready to go. They recognized me as an impostor. They glared.

Mrs McGuiness said, 'Girls, let's welcome Rachel Bennett to the sisterhood.'

I thought, great! I've got more sisterhood at home than I can handle.

If Mrs McGuiness' enthusiasm was any indication, our expedition was to be exciting beyond all measure of expression. Turns out, we walked across the street and stared at a ditch.

She said, 'This, girls, is a very impressive example of a beaver lodge. Can anybody tell me what kind of animal a beaver is?'

Kelly Renfrew raised her hand and waited to be called upon. She said, 'A mammal?'

Mrs McGuiness was very pleased. 'Excellent, Kelly. Yes, a beaver is a mammal. A beaver is also classified as a rodent and, not just any rodent, but the world's second largest rodent!'

I asked, 'What's the largest?'

'That would be a good question for you to research when we get back to school, Rachel.'

'Don't you know?'

'This is your first time here, I understand. But I believe what you'll find is that these expeditions aren't about what I know and don't know but what *you* can discover. It will give you a sense of empowerment to be curious about the world and then seek your own answers. We also have a policy about speaking out of turn. Raise your hand and wait to be called on.'

'Would you like for me to give you a hint?'

Mrs McGuiness directed the conversation back to the 'dynamic construction of the dams'.

I took a moment to survey my situation. I was standing by the side of a busy road getting exhaust fumes blown up my short green skirt while Mrs McGuiness read beaver facts from a flashcard. I couldn't see any beavers and that clag of sticks and mucky water wasn't anything new. I noticed that Holly Purvis was fingering the buttons and badges crowding her sash. She stared at me as if I'd just brought pox into the tribe.

I raised my hand, waited to be called upon and asked, 'When will we start selling the cookies?'

Mrs McGuiness said that I was getting a little ahead of myself.

'Is there a prize for the one who sells the most?'

'I think you're missing the point of the outing.'

I didn't get my Beaver Badge that day and Mrs McGuiness called Mother. She told Mother that I wasn't mature enough yet to handle Girl Scouts. She suggested that I try the Brownies first.

Mother thought Brownie uniforms were hideous and that was the end of that.

I'd rather be in bars than behind them.

One year after I relieved Daniel of his prenuptial responsibilities, I was still single.

By way of celebration, I bought a chair.

I didn't have much furniture, mainly scraps left from one divorce or another. Giving up hard goods without contest served many purposes.

It was a good way to:

1. Cut losses and start over.
2. Apologize for gross inadequacies (both real and imagined).
3. Prevent oversentimentality about a relationship gone wrong.

It's hard to wear rose-coloured glasses while remembering how an ex-husband carted off everything from the Kitchen-Aid mixer to the lavender sachet from your lingerie drawer.

When I bought the chair a clerk at the register asked, 'Are you going camping?'

'No.'

'Oh, is it for your kids?'

'No.'

She stared. I stared. She hesitated for just a second longer and said, 'You do know it's a blow-up chair, right?'

'It occurred to me when I read this,' I said, pointing to the box: INFLATABLE. DO NOT PUNCTURE. OPEN CAREFULLY.

She avoided eye contact and sang along with the radio during the remainder of our transaction which I thought was a pleasant enough way to avoid further retail tension.

She asked, 'Do you need help getting your purchase to the car?'

I shook my head no.

She said, 'Have a blessed day.'

And it was the tone she used! I wanted her to take that back and I stood a little too long trying to think of ways to get her to retract it that wouldn't get me arrested. Choking her out was all that came to mind. *Have a blessed day.* I think more than anything one of the undercurrents constantly pulling at me, not unlike gravity, is the hypocrisy that exists under society's thin veneer. *Have a blessed day.* I feel fear every time I hear that. It's like being in a zombie movie and not being sure which of your friends is infected until you're locked in the safe house with them and slowly but surely they reveal themselves to be plague-ridden. *Have a blessed day.*

★ ★ ★

The first time I sat in my new chair, it developed a slow leak.

I was thumbing through the latest issue of *Entrepreneur Magazine*, trying to find my father's 'alias articles', when I realized the chair was hissing at me. I made a mental note to get a patch kit but in the meantime I kept the electric air pump close at hand.

My father is a long-time contributor to *Entrepreneur Magazine*. I call them his 'alias articles' because he doesn't want the general public to know (general public = board members and stockholders in his own companies). My father's motto: Anonymity is like a warm blanket.

His secretary, Gloria, always mails me a copy and I try to figure out how many times my father's been quoted. He might show up as International Businessman, Javier Fuentes or Stock Analyst, Jill Millbrook. I have an 89% average picking him out.

In *Advice to Up-and-Coming Entrepreneurs,* I was surprised to see a picture of 'former Alabama bailiff, Eddie Walker' and his chocolate-coloured Lab. They were sitting on the steps of a private jet, supposedly getting ready for a trip to the coast of

France where his family was vacationing. Eddie had invented a newfangled cup holder, branded it to the bottling companies and marketed millions of them in packaging promotionals.

Thinking about Eddie living large gave me reason to pause and consider my own financial situation.

I had to face facts about money.

I didn't have any.

I walked away from my last divorce with a healthy settlement which would have been fine if I hadn't also lost my job and spent a small fortune courting disaster with Daniel. Turns out, I acquired another nasty souvenir from him. This one involved prescription pain medication.

Being addicted to drugs is expensive.

Being addicted to drugs while also taking a smorgasbord of antidepressants, antipsychotics and anti-anxiety medication is a diet I wouldn't recommend.

I was living the life of a recluse, going out only to satisfy my compulsion for narcotics and Szechuan Spicy Trio. I craved odd combinations of food, sometimes boiled rice with pancakes and maple syrup or link sausage dipped in chocolate. I washed it down with gallons of lemonade. The enamel on my teeth suffered as much as anything else.

I was my own worst enemy: rebellious child *and* over-indulgent mother.

I could elaborate about my degenerative mental condition. I could try to explain the depths of my loneliness. But that's all crunchy, candy coating. It was the lack of money that pushed me to seek help. I don't know what I dreaded more, my father finding out that I had a drug problem or finding out that I was broke. The only reason he hadn't already thrown me a life preserver was that he didn't know I'd lost my job. But Julie knew. It was only a matter of time before it became public knowledge.

★ ★ ★

For almost ten years I worked at a university within walking distance of my house.

I got fired for conduct unbecoming.

The beginning of the end started with a student, Hunter Lowell. He left a note taped to my office door.

The note read: *I regret to say that my grandmother has suffered cruelly at the hands of old age and her troubles are now compounded by a recent stroke. It's simply a matter of priorities. Do with me what you will but I won't be available for final exams. I feel I must be at the hospital should my grandmother take a turn for the worse. Yours truly, Hunter.*

I read it to three of my colleagues while we ate pasta salad. They laughed so hard one of them nearly choked. Another one threatened to pee her pants.

Donna Glom, a professor of Comparative Literature, managed to gain control long enough to explain that Hunter Lowell was racking up quite a reputation for burying grandmothers. Seems he'd written the same letter, verbatim, to several other professors.

She said, 'Let me see… with another impending funeral, that brings the grandmother body count to seven.' She put the back of her hand to her forehead and said, '*Alas. Alack. Do with me what you will, Professor Bennett.*'

I gave Hunter Lowell an Incomplete. If he didn't schedule a make-up exam the Incomplete would automatically downgrade to Fail. He wasn't pleased.

For most people that would have been end of story. Not for me.

When finals were finally over, I collected essays from my last class and set them free.

I left my office about half past two, said goodbye to Donna Glom and walked to my car. It was a provokingly perfect afternoon. Cherry blossoms scattered on a light breeze. A fringe of tender green leaves agitated the periphery, teased my eyes into looking directly at the sky: defiant blue.

On the way home I got a call from Daniel. He said, 'I'm stuck here at work and there's no way I can get home in time.'

'In time for what?'

'A dude is supposed to be there at five-thirty.'

'A dude? Daniel, why would you do that? Do you even know this person? I'm here alone and you've got a drug dealer dropping by the house?'

'For fuck's sake, PHONE!'

'I don't care who hears me.'

'Well, I do! Don't freak out. The guy is fine. It won't be a problem. Just be cool.'

'I've had a bad day. I don't want to do this.'

'I've had a bad day too.'

'And?'

'You're not the only one who has bad days, Rachel.'

'And? That still doesn't mean I feel like doing this. How do you plan on paying him?'

'Do you have any money?'

'I do, but...'

'I'll pay you back.'

'You won't.'

I pulled into the driveway and made my way into the house as Daniel made small talk. I hardly had time to put my things down when there was a knock at the door. It startled me a bit because I knew that he must've watched me come into the house. I told Daniel in a whisper, 'Hang on a second. I think he's here.'

I opened the door and standing there was Daniel's supplier, Hunter Lowell.

He smiled. I didn't.

By Monday morning the Dean was reading an anonymous letter claiming that I solicited controlled substances from a student. It's lucky for me that I knew the Dean was having an affair with a sophomore or I would have been more than fired.

★ ★ ★

In the thick of all this, Emma said to me, 'Don't worry. That which doesn't kill you only makes you stronger.'

I gave it my best shot but only managed to graze her left hand with a serving fork.

★ ★ ★

Julie found out that I was unemployed because she is married to a particle physicist named Frank Morgenstern.

I've never had a problem with Frank. He's always seemed blissfully ignorant of Julie's faults and is the happiest person I've ever met. He was also extremely intelligent and smelled of pine cleaner. I don't know if the two things were related. It wasn't an unpleasant odour just persistent. Julie said that Frank washed his hands frequently.

Frank was friends with Morton Healy, another high energy physicist. I knew Morton because one of my colleagues in the English Department, Donna Glom, married him three weeks after he gave her 'a good seeing to' at the New Year's Eve faculty party.

Morton is how Julie found out that I was unemployed.

Julie came to the university with Frank, who was trying to help Morton acquire federal funding for a particle accelerator. She wasn't planning on seeing me until Morton let slip that I no longer worked for the university.

When I answered my cell phone, Julie asked, 'What are you doing?'

I said, 'Eating a peanut butter sandwich. What are you doing?'

'I'm on campus with Frank. I'll meet you at your office.'

'I'm not there right now. I came home for lunch.'

'I don't mind. I'll wait for you.'

'No. I'll meet you at Coffee Casa on University Boulevard.'

Julie laughed and said, 'I'll be there in ten.'

Once we were seated, Julie used a spoon to push the froth of her skinny latte to one side so that it would cool. She said, 'I planned to jerk you around a while about this job thing but, to be honest, I'm already bored with it.'

'What job thing?'

'Don't bother, I know. The question is: does Dad know?'

'I haven't told anybody.'

Julie said, 'Ce sera notre petit secret.'

'Oui, en français s'il te plaît. Our little secret.'

* * *

Inside joke:

Two days after Julie's twelfth birthday, I knocked on Mother's bedroom door and she answered wearing a full face of make-up, a natural blue fox fur coat, a silk nightgown and a pair of Vanity Fair red velvet mules. It was after midnight.

I said, 'I think Julie…'

Mother clapped her hands in my face and said, 'En français, s'il vous plaît.'

'No. Please hurry. I think Julie…'

'En français!'

'You don't understand French!'

She slammed the door in my face.

I called 911.

When the paramedics got there, Mother came out of her room and demanded to know what was going on.

I said, 'Les ambulanciers pensent que Julie a besoin d'une appendicectomie.'

Mother said, 'What?'

* * *

The worse my situation got, the worse I made it.

I couldn't afford cable so I made rabbit ears out of bent coat hangers. Even then all I could pick up was public television. I would stay in my apartment all day, sitting in my inflatable chair, watching Sesame Street, eating dry cereal and waiting for a dealer named Sarah to bring me tranquillizers.

The last time she came by my house I tried to pay her with a waffle iron and a pack of padded, scented coat hangers.

She said, 'What the fuck is this?'

I said, 'It's a very nice waffle maker and, hey, don't underestimate these coat hangers. You can hang your sweaters without the shoulders getting misshapen.'

She said, 'Misshapen? I'll be misshapen if I go back with this trash. Do me a favour: lose my number.'

'You want to stay a while and just talk?'

'Take a bath.'

I never saw her again.

Through all of it I still thought: something will happen. Things will get better. I won't have to call my father. He'd already bailed me out more times than I could count.

Once before, when I was facing a mountain of financial debt, I considered filing for bankruptcy. I went so far as to speak with an attorney. He advised me of my legal position and the havoc I would wreak on my credit history should I take the bankruptcy route. The same day I met this attorney, I got a call from my father.

Turns out lawyers are part of a tighter knit community than one might expect. I thought they were out severing brake lines, pouring sugar in gasoline tanks and poisoning each others' favourite pets. But, no, at least not all the time. The lawyer I met knew somebody who knew somebody else who knew, etc… It took less than two hours for my father's personal legal counsel to know the skinny on my financial woes.

When my father called, there was a noise in the background that I couldn't quite make out. I asked, 'Where are you?'

'I am on the Andaman Sea, Phang Nga Bay.'

'Where's that?'

'Between Phuket Island and Thailand. More importantly, where are *you*?'

'I'm sitting in my car while some guy does a lube express.'

'Pardon me?'

'I'm getting the oil changed in my car.'

'I don't have time to argue with you. So, simply, no bankruptcy. We've *done* broke before and we aren't going to do it again. Let Gloria know how much you need and I'll take care of it.'

There was a pause in the conversation. He asked, 'Are you still there?'

'Yes, still here. Who is that I hear talking?'

'Rachel, I can't understand why you've got to be so damned stubborn. Why do you get yourself into situations like this?'

I could hear another man speaking close to the phone, issuing various warnings: 'tell her this' and 'tell her that'.

I asked again, 'Dad, who is that?'

'It's Miles and he's just as upset as I am that you're considering such a thing.'

Miles Hopkins was my father's lead attorney and, how shall I say… confidante.

Miles said, 'I think she enjoys being perverse about these things.'

My father said, 'Why won't you just let me help you and give you the things that I want to give you? Things you need. Do you enjoy being intentionally perverse?'

'You're breaking up. I can hardly hear you.'

'Not surprising.'

'Bad connection.'

'Do as I say. Call Gloria.'

★ ★ ★

Gloria has been my father's secretary since before I was born.

She knew more about the family than the family knew about itself.

I've harboured fantasies that my father would leave Mother and run away with Gloria. I once asked him if he found Gloria attractive.

He said, 'Yes. She is a very together, nice-looking woman.'

I said, 'A bit of a sex kitten, don't you think?'

'A sex kitten?'

'Yes, in a sort of dark-haired, vampish-homemaker, I can rock your world *and* bake oatmeal cookies kind of way.'

He said, 'Rachel, darling, you push me closer to an aneurism every time you say something like that.'

Regretfully, they never ran away together.

There's something to be said for having the right regrets in life but I suspect the regret was all mine, not theirs.

★ ★ ★

When my father said we'd *done* broke before, there was a reason for that.

It wasn't because we didn't have money.

It was more a self-imposed poverty.

My father's parents died of carbon monoxide poisoning. There was a gas leak at their home in upstate New York. The investigation concluded that they went to sleep in their respective Lazy Boy recliners, Grandmother doing the TV Guide crossword puzzle and Grandfather nursing a snifter of Henri IV Dudognon, without any idea that their lives were in danger. There was no indication of foul play or suicide.

My father inherited somewhere in the neighbourhood of 40 million dollars.

There was a bit of a catch to the financial situation. Even though my father had a young bride in tow, he was proud. He insisted on living modestly until he could make his own fortune.

Julie and I weren't born at the time and we didn't hear this story until much later.

My father's decision to stay out of the inheritance was not because he was a selfish man. On the contrary, he made sure Mother had a healthy allowance. The only caveat: don't flaunt it.

We grew up in a low-slung, ranch-style house with as much personality as a box of saltine crackers. The neighbourhood was blue collar. Most of the mothers worked day jobs and most of the fathers worked shifts, their bedroom windows blacked out with aluminium foil so they could sleep during the day.

Mother enjoyed secret luxuries. Her bedroom windows were blanketed with heavy 18th-century fabrics, tassels and ties. She had a Louis XV bronze-mounted, tulipwood vitrine upon which she displayed her collection of marble mantel clocks and French bisque cherubs. She had a Viennese jewellery cabinet for all the fine charms she could only wear indoors. One Bulgari necklace was worth more than our house.

We were on a strict 'Don't Ask Don't Tell' policy as regarded money. We knew better than to ask too many questions or to complain that the rest of the house looked like a shrine to the Salvation Army. It was something we didn't discuss. Our life was a strange mix of modesty and extravagance, something the other kids in the neighbourhood couldn't resist pointing out. Mother might as well have slathered us in honey and kicked over a bee hive.

In an effort to fit in, I put aluminium foil over our bedroom windows. When Mother saw it, she pulled a genuine Joan Crawford. Even though I wasn't a religious child, I said a prayer of thanks that there weren't any wire hangers in the closet.

She asked, 'What would make you do this?'

'I didn't think it was a big deal.'

'Do you think we're poor white trash?'

I hesitated for a moment and said, 'Yes?'

Mother took the response as if I'd landed a solid blow to the bread box. She said, 'You ungrateful girl! Just you wait till your father gets home.'

She received a box of truffles from France and was sufficiently distracted when my father got there. She forgot to mention the foil incident. I told him myself.

'I put foil on our windows and Mother was furious.'

My father looked at me over the top of his glasses and said, 'I'm surprised you're still in one piece.'

'She asked me if I thought we were white trash.'

'And?'

'And, I said yes.'

'Why would you say such a thing?'

'She asked me if I *thought* we were and, you know how it is, I couldn't tell if it was a definitely yes or definitely no question.'

He laughed and pulled me up close.

He smelled like oranges and cinnamon.

★ ★ ★

Drugs are an inconvenient indulgence.

I could wax philosophical about addiction, the metaphorical and intangible devastations one experiences as a result, but speaking strictly from an 'if P then Q' stance, the tangible fallout isn't a sensible trade-off. I base this opinion not only on the financial wreckage, not only on the physical, not only on the psychological but, plainly and simply: they put my ass in jail.

The police raided an apartment where I spent the night with a couple of friends. I'd first met them earlier that evening, in the parking lot of a Wal-Mart about twenty-five miles north of my house. I'd used my last ounce of gas getting there and spent my last penny buying pills. When I couldn't get my car started, one of the fellows came over and, in his best broken English, invited me to come to their casa.

I said, 'Gracias.'

I stayed for dinner and drank warm Tequila until I passed out on the floor. I woke up just before dawn with a flashlight shining in my face. A cop pulled the bag of pills from between my breasts.

I said, 'I'm American!'

He said, 'Me too!'

Then he cuffed me and took me to jail.

★ ★ ★

I was questioned, booked, printed, photographed, stripped, searched, showered, de-loused, dressed and put in a cell with other clean, dirty people. I felt like a drenched cat being dragged across shag carpet.

One of my cellmates said, 'I'm Alicia.'

'Nice to meet you, Alicia.'

'They've already served breakfast.'

'I could do with a couple of Vicodin.'

'Don't have any Vicodin but I got half of a Snickers.'

I wasn't in the mood for small talk. I tried to appear busy with my own thoughts until it became impossible to ignore the woman next to me. Alicia tried to comfort her.

Alicia looked at me and said, 'This is Connie. She's missing her babies.'

I raised my eyebrows and nodded. 'Connie's got two little girls staying with her mama and the boy is with his grandma.' In a quieter voice she said, 'They all three got a different daddy.'

Connie said, 'It's been better than two months now since I seen them. It ain't fair.'

I'm all about feeling sympathetic to the plight of a mother and child torn apart by circumstance but when Connie said 'two months', I felt a self-concerned panic surge through my body. If she hadn't seen her kids in two months, I wondered how long she had been in jail. I then wondered how long I would be in jail. The prospect of being locked up with Connie and Alicia for two months didn't sound so good.

I asked, 'What did you do to get stuck in here for two months?'

'I've only been in since Wednesday.'

'Wednesday? This past Wednesday?'

Alicia looked over to me and nodded on Connie's behalf.

I said, 'That's only three days. Why haven't you seen your kids in two months?'

Alicia said, 'Connie hasn't got custody of her kids right now. She's had a hard time. Her mama only just now got the two little ones back from the State care.'

Connie wasn't crying any more. She turned around and raised her shirt. 'Can you see them?' She pointed to a tattoo on the small of her back. 'See those four names?'

'Yeah.'

'Those are my kids' names and I put that fourth one on there even though he died.'

I could smell Connie and I'd had just about enough of her backend in my face. I said, 'That's a nice gesture.'

'It's not just a gesture. I did it so they'd know. I want them to know how much I love them.'

'Well, nothing says "I love you" like body art.'

Connie was getting closer and I felt a primitive urge to defend my personal space. Alicia must have sensed the tension because she pulled Connie away. They sat on the other side of the cell, whispering and looking at me.

I imagined ways to get my bag of pills back.

* * *

Sometime during that blur of a bastard morning, I was allowed to make a phone call.

I called Gloria.

When she answered the phone, I tried to say hello but all I could hear was a recorded voice requesting permission for the call. 'This is an automated serviced from InmateAnnounce. You have just received a call from an inmate at the Cullman County Jail. If you wish to immediately decline this call and block further calls from the same number press star sixty-two. Should you accept this call you will be charged a dollar fifty and one dollar for each additional minute. Press star one to accept. Press star two to decline.'

I heard two tones. I wasn't sure if she accepted or refused.

'Gloria? Are you there?'

Silence.

Finally, she said, 'Rachel?'

'Yeah. It's me.'

'Are you in jail?'

'I'm messed up, Gloria. I'm really messed up. I lost my job and I've been taking too many pills and the policed raided an apartment I was in…'

'Stop. Don't say anything else over the phone. Did they hurt you?'

'No.'

'Somebody will be there as soon as possible.'

'I'm sorry. I'm so sorry. I'll make it right, ok? Please don't be disappointed in me. I'll make it right. I promise.'

'Enough of that, kiddo. We'll get you sorted.'

It wasn't long until a pack of my father's attorneys descended. They were frothing at the mouth to be part of the search and rescue team that brought Daddy's Little Girl home.

Luckily, the powers that be weren't put off by all the Armani aftershave and pinstriped power suits. The sheriff and the district attorney had a 'share the wealth' policy for first-time offenders. They let us know there was wiggle room and we didn't waste the opportunity to set the wheels of small town politics in motion.

Transactions were made. I was dusted off, patted on the head and sent home. The sheriff told me to keep my nose clean.

A pint's a pound, the world around.

Blood is thicker than water, but not by much.

We had a housekeeper named Minnie. We weren't allowed to call her a housekeeper not because Mother was interested in elevating Minnie's station in life but because my father didn't want the neighbours to know that we had 'staff'. Mother told the neighbours that she was mentoring Minnie and that she had previously been languishing in a halfway house for heroin addicts. In actuality, Minnie graduated from Duke University cum laude. We weren't allowed to mention that either.

I asked Mother why she would rather the neighbours think we had a heroin addict in the house rather than a housekeeper and she said, 'Don't stereotype, Rachel.'

Minnie did more than keep the house tidy, she served as a spa practitioner and masseuse. She spent a great deal of time applying non-abrasive sloughing lotion to various parts of Mother's body. Not to mention frequent detoxing, cleansing, buffing and polishing sessions.

Minnie's Uncle Jeff was a language professor, a retired Yale man who visited the house three afternoons a week. Mother didn't see a point in complicating things so she introduced him as *our* Uncle Jeff. People believed this even though there was no family resemblance either in physical characteristics, temperament or in his appetite for tweed blazers.

* * *

Every night the same thing: dinner together at 6p.m.

Because my father was away on business most of the time that left just us girls. The forced camaraderie left me cold.

Mother fancied herself as a chef. She wasn't. She was forever experimenting with texture. Elaborate production was the name of the game: pink, congealed shrimp salad, turned out of an intricate mould, jiggling like a chubby stripper.

She had a closet full of gourmet cookbooks. There wasn't a single 'simple' recipe in the lot of them. They all called for obscure ingredients. Chinese bayberry from south of the Yangtze River. Fried bamboo worms from Thailand. Soil from the Sankalakhiri mountain range in Malaysia. I would have much preferred a grilled cheese sandwich.

Minnie was a better cook, preparing modest meals (meatloaf, mashed potatoes, creamed corn, baby carrots – that sort of thing). It was rare for her to take over the culinary duties, though. Whenever Minnie cooked Mother ended up flouncing out of the room saying, 'Not every meal needs ketchup and Worcestershire sauce.'

★ ★ ★

Just like the evening meal, going to the grocery store was a ritual.

The only difference was that I looked forward to grocery day.

Sometimes it was the Piggly Wiggly, sometimes it was the A&P but it was always fun. Mother packed us all in the car: me, Phillip, Jack and even Julie. She'd buy us all a cookie from the deli and then disappear into the aisles with a long shopping list. Julie would busy herself in the cosmetics department. We would hang around the magazine section.

The final time we all went out to the grocery store there was some trouble.

The woman who hands out free samples had to chase Jack away from the cheese tray, first of all. She must have ratted us out to the manager because he caught up with us in the stationary aisle. Jack already had five or six car magazines splayed out on the floor. He was being quiet at least. But Phillip was pushing me as fast as he could up and down the aisle on a cart that was half loaded with cartons of Little Debbie cakes.

We were let off with a warning, made to put the magazines back in place, and sent up front to wait for Mother. But then the manager caught Julie making out with one of the produce boys and he caught us stealing prizes from the vending machines.

I hadn't thought of it as stealing. It didn't occur to me to keep the stuff. I only did it because Jack dared me. He didn't think that my hand was small enough to reach inside the door and trip the dispenser. I proved to him that it was.

The manager paged Mother over the intercom. He had all four of us in a line-up by customer service.

He said, 'Ma'am, if you can't keep your children under control when you frequent our establishment then we prefer that you take your business elsewhere.'

Mother said, 'My children? What are you talking about?'

'You've got a ring of sex-crazed felons on your hands, Ma'am. May I ask is their father absent from the home?'

'Who in the hell do you think you're talking to?'

'Language, please. I will ask you to remain calm or I'll be forced to involve the authorities.'

'Language my ass! Let's get something straight here, these are *not* my children.'

Julie pointed back and forth between me and her and said, 'We are.'

Mother said, 'Well, yes those two are. But not *all* of them. My hips are far too narrow to ever be responsible for him.' She pointed to Phillip.

I said, 'Mother!'

By this time the store manager was on the intercom again. He said, 'Security to the front of the store.'

When Mother finally got us home she swore she'd never take us out together again. The last I heard of it she was crying to Minnie, recounting events. She said, 'They must have thought I was some low-life redneck with a litter of squirrelly-looking children.'

★ ★ ★

For all I knew my father spent his time in Peru selling shower curtain rings.

He could be a very playful man, genuinely tender and sweet but there were aspects of his life that he insisted remain private. He said, 'Business is business. Home is home.' That's why when he told us that we were rich, I wasn't sure how to respond.

Minnie was outside, slapping the (locked) sliding glass door and telling me that the Boogie Man was going to get me if I didn't let her in. Julie had flushed Phillip's hamster down the toilet and flooded the place. The hamster wasn't dead when he went in but he was when he came out. Mother was conditioning her hair with a mayonnaise treatment and trying to get a plumber to come out and stop water from boiling out of the toilet.

After my father turned off the water main he gathered us around the dining-room table and said, 'I've looked forward to this day since before you girls were born. I've imagined what I would say to you but, now that the time has finally arrived, I feel stifled, silenced by an uproar of raw emotion.'

He lowered his head as if he were praying. He picked a piece of lint from his double-breasted lapel and continued.

'It gives me a primal sense of satisfaction like a hunter returned from the kill to sustain, to nourish his young. Girls! You must set goals for yourselves. Be strident. Be determined. Passion without vigour, without drive is like a lukewarm bath. Decide what you want from life and let nothing, nothing at all stand in your way.'

The plumber arrived. Minnie showed him into the dining room. He had an assistant with him who was wearing a t-shirt which read: Pickles.

The plumber said, 'We don't take credit cards.'

Nobody said anything.

The plumber said, 'Which one of you is paying? It'll have to be cash or check. Cash is best.'

Mother snapped her fingers at Minnie and said, 'Would you please handle that for heaven's sake.'

Minnie said, 'Yes ma'am.' She showed them out.

My father was irritated. He was scribbling on a pad of paper which, when he began again, he read from.

'Personal goals are paramount. It is on this day that I can proudly say: I've reached mine. Mother had her doubts. My father had his doubts. They were sceptical that I would ever achieve greatness. My father said I was a poor sportsman and my weak chin annoyed him to great distraction. But, I have matched his fortune to the penny, to the penny, I say! Things are not always what they seem. Get your things girls, we're moving.'

Mother was out of the room before he'd finished. She was shouting for Minnie to bring the suitcases.

Julie said, 'Graças a Deus, finalmente.'

My father looked pleased.

He looked at me and said, 'Well?'

I hesitated then said, 'Way to go.'

He laughed. 'Is that all you've got to say?'

'What about Phillip and Jack?'

'Don't worry about Phillip and Jack, darling. We aren't moving *that* far away. You'll still see them.'

We took a limousine over to the fancy part of town. Mother sat still, poised as if she were deposed nobility being restored to the throne. Julie seemed very composed, as if she had considerable experience with limousines. My attention oscillated between the sunroof and the wet bar.

The new house was a hulking mass of sophistication and limestone. It was originally commissioned in 1929 by a Scottish industrialist.

There was massive renovation underway. Landscape teams were restoring the gardens and rebuilding rock walls and pathways and tradesmen were inside tearing down walls and putting in a professional-grade kitchen. When Mother saw the appliances, I thought she was going to faint. But we weren't there long before there was trouble. Mother had a dizzy spell after she got in a heated discussion with the site manager about hedge placement.

She needed a moment to lie down but there were no beds yet. So we only stayed in the new house for about an hour (long enough for Mother to snag a copy of the blueprints and architectural plans and to ask why she hadn't been provided a hard hat of her own) before my father decided we were all due a vacation. We flew to New York City and lived in the Four Seasons hotel while the house was completed.

Whispery-Go-Feely.

When I got home from jail, I opened the door to my house and was knocked back by the smell of cat litter.

I didn't have a cat.

I sprayed air freshener which made the place smell like cat litter in a summer orchard.

There was a message on my answering machine from my father. 'Will be back in the US early tomorrow. Please don't leave the house. Call your mother if you need anything before I get there.'

I hadn't spoken to Mother in years. Not since she tried to poison my father with lawn fertilizer. She thought he was sleeping with another woman. *Because* he didn't die, he was able to explain to her that he was actually sleeping with another man. Mother seemed more capable of dealing with that. Instead of pressing charges for attempted murder (Miles, lead attorney, confidante and now admitted lover advised against a scandal), my father agreed to a trial separation. They'd never bothered with a divorce.

Everything was pretty much as I'd left it: a mess. I sat down in my inflatable chair and rolled onto the floor. I crawled to a patch of sunlight coming through the windows and thought it best to be still. I didn't get up for quite some time. It reminded me of how Phillip and Jack's dog, Winston, would lie in a sunny spot on the carpet. I loved the way his paws smelled. I loved that he was a goon. But most of all, I loved the idea that he loved me unconditionally.

I thought about how we used to play football with Winston. How when Phillip and I were out of breath, Jack would keep playing. He'd run until he was wet with sweat.

I thought about holding Winston in my lap, too heavy, too

hot, too big, clumsy happy thing; certainly not a lapdog. But there we were driving down I65. I remember the slight smell of yeast from his ears. He didn't know what was about to happen. He didn't know he was about to die.

It was me that looked over at the guy on the Harley that Sunday afternoon. I looked at him and he waved at me. I waved back and that's when Jack floored it.

I whispered, 'Jack.'

Images shuffled through my mind. Even after all these years my skin still expected his touch. I imagined how different this house would be if Jack was still with me.

* * *

From my vantage point on the floor, all I could see was a wall of cardboard boxes. Still packed, some opened with newspaper spewing from the top. I thought about that morning, the shame my father must have felt when Gloria told him. I wanted to prove that I wasn't useless. I wasn't bad. I decided, right then and there, lying on that floor with my guts rumbling and my head splitting, that I would turn my life around.

I decided to unpack.

I would start over. I didn't need Jack or anybody else.

The first box I went through was full of purses and beaded coasters. The second box was full of hand-blown glass Christmas ornaments. The third box I unpacked was a mix of various things, a bird house, Indian woodblocks and a spoon collection.

Panic.

I started ripping open boxes.

Not a single one of them contained anything worth a damn when it came to setting up house. There were no pots and pans, no dishes, not a single fork in the whole lot. I'd been using the same take-away, plastic sporks since I moved in. What I did find was my grandmother's state spoons.

My grandmother had wanted me to have those spoons when she had never given anybody in our family anything. I held the box to my chest, feeling sick with sentimentality.

I went into my bedroom and opened a silk-covered box. My hands were shaking as I scrabbled around trying to make sure I'd found every single pill. I popped them all in my mouth. Some of the capsule casings started dissolving against my tongue before I could make it to the bathroom sink for a drink of water. I could taste the acidic burn of medication.

I was sure I'd feel better as soon as I had something back in my system.

★ ★ ★

When I woke up, I was in the hospital and my father was looking at me.

I asked him, 'What am I doing here?'

'You tried to kill yourself.'

'No I didn't.'

'You did.'

'I was just sleeping.'

'You've been here for three days.'

I looked up and Mother was standing outside the door. 'What's *that* woman doing here?'

'*That* woman is concerned about you.'

'Did you frisk her for cyanide tablets?'

'Under the circumstances, would you have wished me to find them or not?'

'What's she really doing here?'

'We're all worried about you. Your sister called.'

'Did she ask why you didn't take the opportunity to drown me in a tub of cold water while you had the chance?'

'Don't talk like that. Julie loves you.'

'Julie loves me? She put fire ants in my bed, slept with my second husband and told our therapist that I was a sexually active ten-year-old.'

'Well, you know it doesn't matter. We'd still love you just the same even if you were.'

'I wasn't!'

'We all cry for help in different ways, darling.'

I looked back to the door and said, 'I can't tell if she's looking at me or looking at her reflection in the glass. She's smiling. My bet's on the glass.'

'Your mother and I are thinking of trying again.'

'Well, there you go! I knew she wasn't here just to see me. She can't stand hospitals. It's the fluorescent lighting. It does *terrible* things to her complexion.' I looked back at Mother, who was attending to some manicure malfunction. 'Anyway, I thought you were gay?'

'Only sometimes.'

★ ★ ★

I left the hospital. I went home long enough to get a bag of clothes, a few non-threatening toiletries and that was me, off to rehab.

My father said he would take care of everything.

Gloria booked me into a 'get yourself off drugs while playing tennis and enjoying a warm rock massage' retreat called Whispering Oaks. Once at rehab, it didn't take long to realize that I was going to need more pills to keep from bludgeoning someone as an antidote to the touchy-feely, I'm-alright-you're-alright self-help nonsense.

Whispering Oaks boasted a claim to fame because a handful of B-list actors had visited there on the road to wellness. Most of them had agreed to rehab to avoid a prison sentence. Most people just want to be saved from the consequences of their vices.

The place was founded by a one-time actor, Lawrence McDermott. He was a child star turned awkward, unemployable teen, turned petty criminal, heroin addict. Some might argue: a natural progression. Lawrence wrote a self-help book called *Larry Aloud*. It had run up the New York's Best Seller List. He did the talk show circuit and then, sometime after he was on the David Letterman Show, he was arrested for disturbing the peace.

Lawrence beat the hell out of himself in a hotel room. By the time help arrived, he'd done a fair old job.

Lawrence went to Massachusetts and stayed with his Aunt Marjorie. He never left. He took what money he still had and with financial assistance from Marjorie, bought a Tudor-style home in the Berkshires. And, as some people are prone to do, he assumed that since he had grappled with addiction of various flavours it qualified him to help others facing similar problems.

* * *

My induction ceremony was conducted by Bradford and his Stepford wife, Carrie.

They were high on life and weren't at all squeamish about beating a little lost lamb about the head and shoulders with a happy stick.

They made an alarmingly perfect couple. They smiled a lot. I tried to smile along with them but gave up when I got a cramp in my cheek. I watched them closely that first day. They moved in unison and would have made an excellent synchronized swimming team. They completed each other's sentences without provoking annoyance. Each time it happened they nodded, as if their love had just been reconfirmed.

It was all a bit much for me. I imagined them at home, when nobody else was around – the *real* Bradford and Carrie. I could envision Bradford decked out in an old-school wrestler's costume, chasing Carrie around the house begging her to spank him with a hairbrush. Squeal! I felt more comfortable with this image than the one they presented.

The induction was a complete drain of my sensibilities. They explained that 'addiction' was an ugly, unproductive word and preferred to use the phrase: prolonged, unhealthy preoccupation.

I asked, 'Will I be de-occupied when we're done?' I laughed. They didn't.

Bradford explained how my preoccupation would be treated with kindness and love and understanding. There would be medication to ease the withdrawal symptoms. There would be group therapy, detoxifying dietary measures, hypnosis sessions, meditation, yoga and massage. I would be called upon to re-dedicate myself on a daily basis to healing and understanding by joining in a group ceremony: Lighting Candles of Commitment. Each morning I was to wake with a positive vocalization, a curative chant to promote well-being and strength of spirit. I couldn't think of my own so they let me draw one out of the inspirational chant hat.

They inspected my travel bag and made the following exceptions.

Carrie opened a black purse and found my stash of ink pens. I hadn't officially counted but I would guess there were over three hundred. She said, 'Have you been diagnosed as obsessive compulsive?'

I said, 'Uh-huh.'

She said, 'If I let you keep the pens, do you promise you won't stab anybody including yourself?'

'Yes.'

'Say it for me, please.'

'I promise I won't stab anybody including myself.'

'We've entered into a verbal contract of mutual trust and love. You can keep them.'

Then she found my Connecticut tree quarters. I had twenty-four dollars and fifty cents, all quarters.

She said, 'If I let you keep all this change, do you promise that you won't swallow any of it?'

'Why would I swallow my quarters?'

'If I let you keep them you have to promise me you won't swallow them. It's not uncommon and it's a problem if you do. Promise?'

'Yes.'

'Say it for me, please.'

'I promise I won't swallow change, although, I don't know why you're making such a big deal about it. I've swallowed a lot worse.'

'You should treat your body as you would treat a temple. I can't let you keep the quarters.'

'I won't. I promise I won't swallow my quarters.'

'Good girl. We've entered into a verbal contract of mutual trust and love. You can keep them. The last gentleman we had in here swallowing money had twenty-two pennies in his stomach before we realized what he was doing.'

I'd never thought of swallowing my Connecticut tree quarters but after she said that, I almost couldn't resist the temptation. I was also fixated by the thought of stabbing myself with a pen.

★ ★ ★

At 'phone time', I couldn't think of anybody to call.

I tried Gloria, no answer. I thought about calling Emma but we hadn't spoken since I stabbed her with the fork even though, technically, I only grazed her.

I ended up calling a psychic hotline number that I found in the back of a women's magazine. I used my father's credit card for the charge.

Once I made it through the psychic hotline red tape, listened to all the options, and had been sufficiently hijacked for as much money as they could legitimately steal while leaving me on hold, I was connected to Raymond.

Raymond was busy when he first answered my call. I could

hear the sound of dishes being washed and music playing in the background. At one point, during an uncomfortable lull in the conversation, I asked, 'Is that the Andrews Sisters I hear?'

'No.'

The music stopped. While he finished washing dishes, Raymond told me about how his psychic powers worked. He had an impressive resume. He said, 'I have advised dignitaries and heads of state. I even advised a friend of Julia Roberts' agent to advise Julia to take the role of Erin Brockovich. Not to mention all sorts of powerful people.'

I said, 'And otherwise.' I laughed, seeing as how I was talking to him from from a rehabilitation facility. He didn't see the humour and, upon further reflection, neither did I.

Raymond asked, 'Why are you calling?'

'Do you want me to tell you? I thought you were supposed to guess?'

'You thought wrong. It isn't guessing, thank you very much! It isn't about taking a stab in the dark! There are times when my psychic abilities are a great burden, flippancy will not be tolerated.'

'I'm sorry.'

'Well?'

'Well, what?'

'Why are you calling?'

I told Raymond that I had lost the love of my life, been married and divorced four times, lost my job, spent a small fortune on narcotics and was now in a rehabilitation programme.

He said, 'The cards reveal much. The cosmic plan has many twists and turns. I see great things for you.' He'd turned the Andrews Sisters back up, a bit.

I listened for a while but when I finished out the chorus with emphasis on da Yankee dollah, he turned it down again and said, 'The cards indicate you will benefit from scholarly pursuit. Enrol in a class. Take Russian. Russian translators are in much demand.'

★ ★ ★

I made friends with a girl named Shawna who insisted on wearing a bed sheet on her head so that just a small circle of her face was exposed.

She would only walk to the right side of the hallway.

I personally don't think there was anything seriously wrong with Shawna, excluding the fact that she had a penchant for sniffing glue and sipping gasoline. I think she was bored and liked to shock people. I suspected this when she began relaying elaborate Beowulf rape fantasies and demanding that I call her Shawna the Gift-Giver.

I raised an eyebrow.

She said, 'Too much?'

I said, 'A bit.'

We both laughed.

★ ★ ★

I spent my days at Whispery-Go-Feely talking about my feelings and ingesting a new diet of pills to make coming off the old diet of pills more bearable.

They didn't see a flaw in this logic.

There wasn't a single orifice in my body that wasn't expelling something vile.

Bradford suggested that I take my mind off the severe flu, shakes, nausea, and diarrhoea by taking up a hobby. I suggested swallowing swords but they thought decoupage was a better idea. I spent hours tearing sheets of coloured construction paper into small pieces and then gluing them onto anything that would sit still long enough.

To add insult to injury, it was non-toxic glue. Shawna was disappointed.

They finally broke me. All it took was six hours a day of

decoupage and talk therapy interspersed with bowel movements which registered on the Richter scale. My eyes were red. My lips were split. My ass was chapped. And my insides felt like somebody had ripped me open and lined me with jellyfish. It wasn't necessarily that I didn't still *want* to do drugs. I missed the escape. I just didn't want to be bothered with withdrawal symptoms again.

I thought: stop now or start again and never stop.

I decided to stop.

Once I was done with the gnashing of teeth, rending of flesh and hallucinations, I wasn't quite sure what to do with myself.

★ ★ ★

'Why do you always wear that bed sheet over your head?' I asked Shawna while we were making potholders on mini-looms.

She said, 'It's magic.'

'It's a sheet.'

'It may *look* like a sheet but it is a whole lot more. As long as I wear it doctors can't read my mind.'

'Do you really believe that?'

'Oh, come on, Rachel. What does it matter what I really believe? What's up with you today? Are you trying to psychoanalyse me now?'

'No. I'm just curious.'

After a moment she said, 'It's more like a reminder. It reminds me not to tell them too much, you know? It reminds me to keep some things to myself. People want to be understood. They don't want to be figured out.'

'Maybe if you told them everything they could help you better.'

'Nah, I've tried it before. If you tell them everything they don't help you better they just help you longer. And anyway,' she said, re-adjusting the sheet into cotton pools, 'it's a good look for me, don't you think?'

* * *

One night after a particularly mind-numbing, tell-me-about-your-childhood circle jerk, I snuck out of Whispery-Go-Feely and walked barefoot to a twenty-four-hour pawn and jewellery shop.

I was barefoot because it was policy to check in my shoes during evening hours as a show of trust and a commitment.

Out the window I went. I shimmied down a straggly pine tree and landed in soft mud. I ran across a field, went over a barbed wire fence and onto the main road. Round my neck were all four of my wedding bands, tied together with a piece of string that I'd pulled out of my mattress.

When I finally made it to the shop, I asked the guy behind the counter if he could melt the rings down. He showed me what casts he had: Jesus, a cross, a skull, a rose and a gun.

I told the guy that I'd never shot a gun but, when I was young, I used to answer my sister by saying, 'Okie dokie Annie Oakley.' She would get furious and yell back, 'Don't call me Annie Oakley, you cow!'

The guy was trying to read the writing on my pyjamas as I told the Annie Oakley story but when I stopped talking he said, 'So, you want the gun?'

'Are these all you have got?'

'That's it.'

'I'm not completely sold on any of these. Can you just keep the rings for me?'

'What do you mean *keep them*?'

'I don't want them any more.'

'You're not asking for money?'

'No.'

'Sure, I can do that.'

I left the rings with him and walked back to Whispery.

For the first time in years, I cried.

★ ★ ★

When I got back to Whispering Oaks there was a problem.

I couldn't get back in the way I got out. All the doors were locked. I sat outside on harmony terrace for the rest of the night, waiting for somebody to let me in. My feet were killing me. At one point I became concerned that I had frostbite. But the serenity thermometer by the door said it was 54 degrees. The gods of a mild Massachusetts winter pitied me.

I had dozed off by the time they found me. It was still early morning and I woke to Bradford and Carrie staring at my mud-caked feet. No amount of explaining would convince them that I hadn't betrayed a sacred trust.

Bradford asked, 'Have you been out to hit the pipe?'

'Hit the pipe? Bradford, people don't really talk that way.'

'Blow is a No-Go, Rachel.'

'Blow? I've been to the pawn shop!'

'What have you got left to pawn? You're emotionally bankrupt and your word is worthless.'

'Could you lose the tough love one-liners and just speak normally?'

'How's this? You're going home.'

'I'm not done yet.'

'Yes, you are. We're already packing your bags.'

'You can't just throw me out of here. I've paid a shitload of money to be here.'

'Read your contract. We can and we are. Rules are rules. Is there somebody we can call for you?'

Gloria picked me up. She said, 'You look better than you have for ages.'

I think she meant it.

What about a duck?

A neighbour once told me: If it walks like a duck, quacks like a duck and looks like a duck – it must be a duck.

What she meant to say is: I think your father is homosexual.

As a matter of course, that was a true statement but the neighbour had no evidence other than: unreciprocated flirtation.

Her name was 'Ginger' Maddox and I heard her tell my father on more than one occasion that it was a nickname she earned for being a *real* redhead. Ginger lived next door in a restored Spanish-style *hacienda*, as she called it.

Not long after we had settled in to the new house I overheard her say, 'Mister Bennett, I sure will be glad when this weather warms up enough for me to sneak over here and have a little skinny dip with you in that big old swimming pool.'

My father said, 'Missis Maddox, there's not enough chlorine in the world.'

I didn't blame Mrs Maddox for trying. My father looked handsome sitting in the sunroom, reading the Wall Street Journal. It wasn't often I saw him in casual clothes. Most often he was smartly dressed either coming or going from one business meeting or another. But he cleaned down real good.

When he did come home for a few days at a time he would get restless and we'd end up wandering out for an adventure. Most of the time he took me to a doughnut shop on the other side of town. It was full of men playing checkers, fighting over fishing tackle and complaining about the coffee. It was a dive but we loved it.

My father was always popular in a crowd. He could strike up a conversation with anybody. He said, 'Rachel, the trick to being a good conversationalist is being a good listener.'

The waitresses there couldn't figure us out. A sharp fellow like that, in a place like that with a little girl in tow, no doubt they were intrigued. They always came around to whisper when my father went to the bathroom, especially the one with the name tag: Samantha.

Samantha asked, 'Honey, your daddy a widower?'

I said, 'I don't think so.'

'He divorced from your mama?'

'No.'

'Why don't she ever come in here with you two?'

'You should be glad she doesn't. She'd expect you to clean whatever that is out from under your fingernails before you served her.'

'Oh, is she prissy?'

'She's got a thing about foodborne disease.'

'Want another doughnut, sugar?'

'No ma'am.'

* * *

Our new house was ridiculously big.

I am not sure all of the nine and a half bathrooms were ever used.

Julie made me select which bedroom I wanted first. My proximity played an integral role in which room she selected. She wanted me as far away as possible which worked out fine because I wanted to sleep in the attic.

Mother fought tooth and nail over the attic space. In her grand scheme the attic was designated sewing room. But my father insisted that I have the room I wanted.

He said to Mother, 'Felicia, you don't need *all* the attic space for a sewing room. I could understand if you wished to open a sweat shop but just a sewing room?'

Mother said, 'I want to make curtains. I need room to make curtains.'

'You don't even know how to sew.'

'That's because I've never had a sewing room.'

'How about I take you to the Rue du Faubourg Saint-Honoré à Paris and you can buy curtains there? Oui?'

'That might be nice.'

I said, 'Faire un compromis c'est l'art de couper un gâteau de manière à ce que chacun croit qu'il a le plus gros morceau.'

Julie said, 'Let them eat cake!'

Mother asked my father, 'What are they saying?'

He said, 'Perhaps we should start measuring windows.'

Turned out that Mother never took that trip to Paris. When she found out Miles was going, she refused. She said that she didn't like the way he looked at her.

Miles and my father went without her.

★ ★ ★

We were surrounded by 'old money'.

Old money doesn't care much for new money.

In an attempt to overcome the stigma associated with being nouveau riche, Mother launched a three-pronged campaign: superfluous spending, charitable contributions and supporting the arts.

In her effort to support the arts she acted on the romantic notion that she would become benefactor to a great artist. The artist: Jim Yancy. Jim suggested that he move into the pool house.

Mother let him.

That's me, gone.

When Gloria picked me up from rehab I felt close to hopeful.

I said, 'I appreciate this. Did I drag you away from something important?'

Gloria said, 'I've been in the area for a couple of days. You should know by now, I always have a contingency plan where you're concerned.'

'This is a nice car.'

Gloria said, 'I'm glad you like it. It's yours.'

'What happened to my car?'

'Your father sold it. Did you know it needed a new transmission?'

'No. I didn't know that.'

She apprised me of the business that my father had taken care of since I'd been away. He'd paid all my bills and credit cards, sold my car, broken my lease and had my things put in an air-conditioned storage facility. I had a wallet full of fresh plastic, a new car and room to run.

Gloria took me back to her hotel suite and said, 'Can you believe this wallpaper? It looks like Laura Ashley threw up in here.'

I said, 'It's enough to induce a seizure.'

She pointed to a complimentary fruit basket and told me to try a pear.

I said, 'They look nice but I'm not hungry right now.'

'Why are you walking like that?'

I said, 'My feet are hurting.'

'It's probably those cheap shoes you're wearing.'

'No, I went out barefoot last night which in hindsight wasn't the smartest thing in the world.'

'Take your shoes off and let's have a look.'

'They'll be fine.'

Gloria pointed to the bed. I knew better than to argue.

My socks were muddy and bloody. Gloria sighed. She pulled up a chair and took off my socks. They were stuck to some of the deeper cuts.

She said, 'They're already getting infected.' She took me into the bathroom and I sat on the edge of the tub while she washed and patted dry my feet. She said, 'Listen to me, Rachel.'

'Ok.'

'Are you listening?'

'Yes.'

'Get in the bed and stay there. I'm going to get some antiseptic and bandages and I want you to do as you're told. You could have used a stitch or two in some of those cuts.'

'I didn't know they were that bad.'

'How could you *not* know?'

She gave me a new cell phone and showed me the playlists she'd made for me. She said, 'I thought you might like this.'

While she was gone I listened to the soothing sounds of babbling brooks, rainstorms and crashing waves. The sound of running water calmed me and made me want to go to the bathroom.

When Gloria got back she bandaged my feet. She had also bought me freshly squeezed lemonade and a bag of Brach's Maple Nut Goodies. 'Maple Nut Goodies! I haven't had these in years. My father used to bring Maple Nut Goodies home from every business trip, just for me. He never forgot. They're my favourite.'

Gloria smiled. 'I know.' I pushed them away.

She said, 'What's wrong?'

'I should have known it wasn't him. Bringing candy home to his daughter wasn't one of his personal goals.'

'Oh Rachel, don't be so hard on everybody. Give yourself a break too while you're at it. Grow up a little bit, darling. The important thing is you got them, isn't it?'

'Did you buy all his gifts for him?'

'Pretty much.'

'Even the cantaloupe-coloured sweater?'

'Especially that. Listen, kiddo, you ok to drive or do you want to spend the night here?'

'I'm fine to drive.'

'Here's the plan then. Directions to the cottage at Martha's are programmed into the satellite navigation. Head that way, ok? You'll have plenty of privacy to clear your head and get your thoughts straight.'

'Are you coming?'

'No, I've got to go. Your father is closing a deal in California and I've flown a sushi chef in from Osaka and apparently there's an issue with customs and sea urchin. Promise me you'll wash your feet with peroxide again tonight and put on fresh bandages. Ok?'

'Ok.'

'Can you give me a smile before I go?'

I smiled.

She left.

★ ★ ★

My father's cottage at Martha's Vineyard wasn't really a cottage.

We just called it a cottage in hopes that it would lend a cosy, home-away-from-home feel to what felt more like an empty bed and breakfast. It was shingled and sprawling and decorated as if *Architectural Digest* might stop by for an impromptu photo shoot at any time. It had six bedrooms, seven bathrooms, a media room and a detached guest house that alone had 1,800 square feet of living space.

I was too restless to sit still for long.

I went to the market.

While there, I heard a familiar voice. I walked around the

corner and saw Eddie, former Alabama Bailiff Eddie. He was arguing with the man behind the cheese counter about a wedge of brie. Eddie was wearing a pink polo shirt and white cotton pants with little blue birds embroidered all over them.

'Eddie?'

He looked back and forth between me and the man behind the counter. He said, 'Yes?'

'Eddie! I can't believe it's you!'

'Do I know you?'

'Sure you do! It's Rachel Bennett from divorce court in Alabama. You gave me free concert tickets.'

He tossed some money over the counter and walked past me. He said, 'Sorry lady, you've got the wrong person.'

He got into a Merc McLaren and left the parking lot, in no particular hurry. I looked back to the man behind the counter, pointed at the cheese and said, 'What's wrong with that?'

'Nothing.'

'I'll take it.'

* * *

When I got back to the cottage there was a car in the driveway. I assumed it was my father.

Turns out, it was Mother.

She was sitting at the kitchen table trying to reprogram the ring on her cell phone. It brought back memories of the day we got our first answering machine. It was a bulky piece of, at the time, modern equipment. She worked herself into a frenzy trying to leave the perfect message. She recorded and played back, recorded and played back 40 times. She was frustrated but at the same time, hypnotized by the sound of her own voice. She even sang a couple of versions. She ended up erasing all the personalized messages and set a computer-generated voice to do the greeting.

I asked, 'What are you doing here?'

She looked up in a very casual way and said, 'I think we should spend some quality time together.'

'Well, quality over quantity, let's get it over with. I'll start. I say: Mother did it in the Conservatory with the Candlestick. Is that right?' I unpacked the groceries.

'That isn't funny.'

'Sure it is.'

'That's between me and your father.'

'No it isn't! You tried to kill him!'

'Don't be so dramatic.'

'You fed him fertilizer!'

'Just a little bit. I only wanted to give him an upset stomach.'

'Mother, I'm not up for this. Just tell me what you want.'

'Is that brie?'

'Yeah.'

'I'll have some of that.'

★ ★ ★

Being with Mother made me want to open a vein.

I tried to think about what I'd learned at Whispering Oaks.

Coping techniques.

Basic life skills.

Healthy displacement.

Cavandoli macrame.

I tried to remember what Bradford said before I left.

While the staff finished packing my belongings and completing expulsion paperwork, I was quarantined to Bradford's office. After severing my commitment to the programme, I wasn't allowed to contaminate the healing environment.

He asked, 'Latte?'

'No thanks.'

'Frappuccino?'

'No.'

Bradford picked up the breakfast menu and asked, 'I could do with a croissant, how about you?'

'Really, I'm fine.'

'Breakfast is the most important meal of the day.'

I said, 'Bradford, listen to me. Please. This isn't necessary. I promise I didn't do anything bad while I was out.'

'If it makes any difference, I believe you.'

'Why are you doing this then? I'm not ready to go. Let me finish the programme.'

'You have finished it. I can't imagine that the Sobriety Diploma will mean that much to you anyway.'

'I'm not ready to leave. I feel like I'm on the cusp of something good and I don't want to ruin it.'

'Of course you do. Rachel, let's be real for a moment. You haven't learned anything from this place that you didn't already know and staying here prolongs the inevitable. You're going to have to get along in the world without insulating yourself against every anticipated hurt. There is nothing exceptional in your capacity to feel pain and to be sad. Tough to hear, sweetheart, I know but truth is, everybody feels fear and anger and anguish some time or the other. You're not unique in that respect. Allow yourself to have feelings, good or bad or sad or happy without assigning guilt. There's no reason to punish yourself for desires or pleasures. Learn to deal with them as an adult, not a child. Learn to cope without harming yourself or trying to mask those emotions with weddings and drugs.'

Whispering Oaks wasn't really a bad place, in fact, it was lovely. I was surrounded by the beauty of the Berkshires, not far from the Hoosic River. Even though I wasn't completely prepared to play along with Bradford's 'happy happy, joy joy' puppet show approach, I do think that he had a genuine interest in helping people. I felt ashamed for not taking it more seriously while I was there.

I was replaying this moment in my head as I sat across from Mother. I watched her eat crackers and cheese. Her phone rang, playing a piercing disco tune.

She said, 'You have got to help me change this thing.' She answered the call and then whispered to me that it was her Chinese herbalist. Mother said, 'I can't understand a single word the woman says.'

I asked, 'Where's she from?'

Mother rolled her eyes and whispered, 'Anaheim, I think.'

Her familiar expressions juxtaposed with the distance I felt between us made me sad. I thought things couldn't possibly get more stressful and then Julie opened the door. Frank was with her.

She said, 'I'm starved.' She sat down next to Mother and started in on the cheese and crackers. She was eating and pretending to listen with interest to the phone conversation. She looked at me and said, 'Are there any olives?'

Frank said, 'Good to see you Rachel. How are you feeling?'

'Fine.'

Mother had managed to find the olives when Julie said, 'I've got news.'

'News, how exciting. Do tell.' Mother handed her the olives. Julie pushed them away.

Julie said, 'For the love of all that's good in the world, Frank, sit down. You know it makes me nervous when you tower.' She looked at Mother and said, 'He's always towering over me. He knows I hate it.'

'Frank, come here and sit down, won't you, dear.' Mother directed him to an uncomfortable wooden stool.

Frank sat down and smiled.

Julie said, 'I am pregnant.'

Mother clasped her hands to her mouth and sighed in what could have been described either as ecstasy or horror.

I asked, 'Who's the father?'

Frank coughed.

Mother asked, 'Would you mind terribly if the baby calls me Felicia?'

I went for a bath.

I filled the tub with hot water and soaked until my fingers and toes were sufficiently poached.

When I came back downstairs Mother said, 'Rachel, I bet you haven't had a decent meal since you've been incarcerated.'

I said, 'I wasn't incarcerated.'

Julie said, 'Actually, you were.'

Mother was opening cabinet drawers. 'I'm going to cook something special. But I am sure the pantry isn't stocked properly.' She was looking around the kitchen for a piece of paper to make a grocery list. Mother was a notorious grocery list maker.

'It's a shame for you, Rachel. Not a decent bite to eat for weeks I bet. Shall we have fish? Fresh fish? There's nothing of any use in this kitchen. I'll need everything.'

I said, 'Meals were prepared by a professional chef who had received two Michelin stars.'

Mother wasn't phased. 'It'll be like old times, just us girls at home, together. And you too, Frank. You haven't seen a pad of paper, have you?'

Julie tore off a scrap of paper from an envelope and handed it to Mother but she wouldn't use it.

'I'll need a whole sheet, dear.'

I said, 'Do we really want things to be like old times?'

Mother assumed the position: exaggerated sigh, dramatic shoulder slump, pinched brow, sorrowful eyes. She said, 'Rachel, you've just returned from weeks and weeks of pampering at a top ranked retreat and yet, here you are, doom and gloom.'

'Fifteen seconds ago I spent the last few weeks incarcerated and now, to hear tell, I was lounging in a resort.'

'Why are you dead set on making everybody miserable?'

Julie said, 'She's always been like that. Why do you expect

anything different?'

'I'm *not* like that and I haven't always *been* like that, whatever *that* is. But ask yourself Julie, why the hell are you even here right now? I'm just out of rehab, trying to figure out a way to take care of myself and you show up along with Mother Murder.'

'Oh please, Rachel, get off it. There's nothing wrong with you. It's just a way for Daddy's precious baby to get more attention and money. It's the oldest trick in the book: fake with the left, jab with the right.'

I said, 'I have no idea what you're talking about.'

'You were out of work and desperate so hey, why not go on a bender so Daddy can play the hero? Sounds like a plan to me.'

Mother said, 'Out of work? I thought you were on sabbatical from the University?'

'No, she got caught trying to buy drugs from a student and they fired her.'

'Dear God! You bought drugs from a student? Why on earth would you do that? Could you not find a legitimate dealer or street person for that kind of thing?'

'The drugs actually weren't for me, like anybody here is going to believe that.'

Julie loved that. 'The drugs weren't for her Mother. That explains everything. No need to worry. The drug addict wasn't buying drugs for herself. I suppose she was shopping early for Christmas.'

Mother carried on. 'I don't know why I doubted my intuition. A mother knows these things but I gave her too much credit. I know her better than she knows herself, Julie. I do. And when she was a child she was forever trying to snow me about one thing or the other.'

I said, 'I'm still in the room. Hello? Stop talking about me like I'm not here.'

'There's no point in trying to have a conversation with you, Rachel, you'll just tell me lies and try to abuse me about whatever imagined injustices you feel. You hold me responsible for things that are your own fault.'

'How am I responsible for you poisoning Dad?'

'See, there you go. Perfect example.'

Julie said, 'There's no point, Mother, stop wasting your time.'

Mother said, 'Frank? Frank?' There was no answer. She said, 'Julie go get Frank. This place needs a Christmas tree and I want him to carry it.'

I asked, 'Are you all staying through Christmas?'

They stared at me but didn't say anything.

I went upstairs to pack.

★ ★ ★

I waited until I thought everybody was asleep but Julie was in the kitchen when I left.

She said, 'What a surprise. I figured you'd be gone by now.'

'I'm surprised you're here at all.'

'Will wonders never cease?'

'Julie, why do you hate me?'

'Why don't you love me?'

I opened the refrigerator. 'There's enough food in here to feed fifty people.'

'Mother is planning a big celebration tomorrow.'

'For what?'

'Maybe she's been plotting for weeks to make your life even more miserable by cooking paella.'

'I don't like paella.'

'You're impossible, you know that? I don't blame Jack for not marrying you.'

We looked at each other for a long moment and then I gathered my bags to leave.

'Rachel, wait. Please wait. I'm sorry. I don't know why I said that.'

'Simple. You wanted to hurt me.'

She met me at the door. 'Don't go. I need you to stay with me.'

'What are you talking about?'

'I want the baby to know you.'

'You don't know me, Julie.'

The kitchen light went on and Frank asked, 'What's going on?'

I opened the door and stepped into the cold.

Julie said, 'Nothing.'

Out of Order.

Mother hosted a party for Jack when he graduated from Cumberland Law School.

I saw the menu and I knew it was going to be a bad night.

Everything was kosher in miniature.

My father was noticeably absent for most of the party.

I finally found him sending text messages in the sunroom.

Mother closed the sunroom to 'guest traffic' because the gardener had left muddy handprints on the window. I told her I would clean them. She said, 'Don't be ridiculous.'

I said, 'I see you've found a place to hide.'

'How's the party?'

'Like Hanukkah on Ice.'

'You've got to give your mother credit for trying.'

'I just heard her ask Jack's mother if she knew that pork was the other white meat.' I sat down next to him and said, 'Are you sorry you married Mother?'

'Please don't ask me questions like that tonight. Between the falafel and blintz loaf, I've got terrible heartburn.'

'I think Jack's going to ask me to marry him.'

'And?'

I was surprised that he had to ask. I said, 'What do you mean?'

'If he proposes will you say yes or no?'

'Do you not like Jack?'

'How could you possibly construe that from a simple question?'

'That's not an answer.'

His cell phone vibrated against the glass coffee table. He read the message and smiled.

I said, 'Miles?'

'How did you know?'

'The same way I know that you're sorry you married Mother.'

He was clumsily thumbing the keypad of his cell phone, trying to reply to Miles. He said, 'Why must they make these things so intolerably difficult to use?'

I said, 'Have you thought about offering Jack a job?'

'I can't say that I have.'

'Why not?'

'What about you? Why don't you work for me? You'd have your choice of just about any place in the world.'

'I'm serious.'

'Me too.'

'Jack graduated top in his class. He's very smart.'

'So are you.'

'We aren't talking about me, Dad. You've got a whole team of lawyers.'

'Yes, so why would I need another one?'

'I had no idea you didn't like Jack.'

'I don't dislike him but Jack strikes me as the type of young man who will look after himself, no matter what.'

'So? He's self-sufficient. Don't you think that is a good quality?'

'There's a fine line between self-reliance and narcissism.'

'Jack isn't narcissistic. He takes my feelings into account. We make decisions based on what's best for us as a couple.'

'I'm not certain how fair it is to either of you to make decisions as a couple before you've learned to make decisions for yourself. I just want you to be happy.'

'I am happy.'

'Compared to what?'

★ ★ ★

My father was right.

Jack was self-involved.

But I was willing to overlook it.

I called it preoccupation passion.

I equated it to an Oxygen Mask Mentality.

Oxygen Mask Mentality: If you are travelling with a companion make sure to securely fit your oxygen mask prior to assisting with theirs.

I found Jack in the game room.

He was shooting pool and telling war stories about junior high football camp.

Phillip threw an olive at me and rolled his eyes.

I asked Jack to come upstairs. There was a unanimous sigh of disapproval from his captivated audience.

Never one to willingly give up the spotlight Jack said, 'Can it wait?'

I put my arm around his waist and said, 'Sure baby, but… you might not want it to.'

The disapproval turned to cat calls and Jack was pleased to rooster his way upstairs with me. 'Excuse me gentlemen. Duty calls.'

Phillip threw another olive at me.

Jack couldn't keep his hands off.

I said, 'Wait a minute. Let's talk.'

He ripped the front of my shirt.

I said, 'For fuck's sake Jack. Wait a minute. I just want to talk to you.'

'What's wrong? Five seconds ago you were all over me.'

'No I wasn't. I just wanted to get you upstairs to talk.'

He was still slowly pawing at me, kissing my neck and wedging his knee between my legs.

'Jack, I need to know if you love me.'

He put my hand down his pants and said, 'If that's not proof enough, I don't know what is.'

'Stop it. I'm serious. We never talk about the future.'

'We talk about the future all the time.'

'I mean our future. When are we going to get married?'

He said, 'Let's fuck and then we'll talk.'

I said, 'I can't. I'm having my period.'

'Well, give me a little executive relief then.'

'No! I want you to talk to me for just a minute.'

He screamed something unintelligible and pushed me away.

I found a jacket to put on over my torn shirt and then went after him.

Phillip stopped me as I was coming down the stairs.

I said, 'Let me go. I've got to find Jack.'

Phillip said, 'He's gone.'

'He's not gone. I just saw him.'

'He took Joanie home.'

'Who the hell is Joanie?'

Phillip said, 'Why did you tell him you were having your period?'

'How did you know that?'

'Jack came running down here pissed off mumbled something to me about you being on the rag and then grabbed Joanie and said he was taking her home.'

'It's none of your business why I told him that.'

'You're finished with your period for this month.'

'How the fuck do you know?'

'I've kept a calendar for years. Any sane man would. I'd rather take a bubble bath with a circular saw than catch you on the wrong day.'

★ ★ ★

Phillip studied at the Nobleman School of Floral Design in Singapore.

I visited him three weeks after Jack got married.

The pair of us stuck out like a sore thumb.

We spent most of our time eating at hawker centres: spicy crab, rice, barbecued stingray, laksa and ice kachang.

It felt good to be with Phillip. It made sense for me to be with somebody who loved me in an uncomplicated way. In fact, it seemed necessary. It was brilliant to rest in the arms of a man who loved me but would rather wear a hair shirt than get to know me in the Biblical sense.

I even went to class with him. He introduced me to his instructor, a woman named Melissa Koh. She humoured me and let me work along with the class on a project of my own. I'd never seen so many beautiful flowers. It seemed a shame to cut them and put them into any kind of arrangement.

Phillip said, 'You've got a good eye.'

I said, 'Pfft.'

'Don't you pfft me. You do.'

'Don't start.'

'I'm serious. Would you learn to take a compliment for God's sake?'

'Don't bring him into it.'

'You know what you should do?'

'Resist the urge to run away?'

'What?'

'Sorry. I have a knee-jerk reaction whenever somebody says: you know what you should do.'

'You should consider doing something like this.'

'Like what?'

'Something creative. A career that allows you to express yourself.'

'The most expressive job I can think of right now is serial killer.'

Phillip came over to my workstation and took a freckled lily from my hand. He tucked my hair behind my ear and said, 'Babysnake, drop it ok? This old routine doesn't work on me. I'm not going to let you soft-shoe your way out of this. There's nothing that says you have to go back to the States to a job teaching freshers composition. I know you're hurt. You will be for a long time. I know.'

He brushed tears from my cheeks, first with the heel of his

thumb and as I cried harder, with the whole of his palm.

'I think Jack will change his mind.'

'He's married. You're going to have to accept that.'

'I don't have to accept anything.'

'Don't be silly. If you keep stabbing at your life with this rusty shank of an attitude then I'm afraid the real Rachel is going to be lost forever.'

'I don't even know who the real Rachel is.'

Phillip said, 'I do.'

★ ★ ★

I have no idea why Phillip calls me Babysnake.

I asked him once and he said, 'It seems appropriate.'

I wouldn't disagree.

★ ★ ★

After Singapore, I went on a nuptial rampage.

I didn't see Phillip much during that time.

I didn't see much of anybody during that time except prospective husbands and divorce attorneys.

But Phillip was busy too.

While I was anaesthetizing myself with one wrong man after another, Phillip opened a floral design studio in New York City.

Child Psychology: A One-Act Play.

Characters:
Dr Marsha Nielson (Dr): Blonde. Child psychologist. Smelled like cotton candy.
Rachel (R): Ten-year-old. Smelled like a ten-year-old.

Dr: Rachel, I know some of these questions may seem embarrassing or difficult to answer but I want you to rest assured that there will be complete confidentiality between the two of us, ok?

R: Ok.

Dr: Do you know what confidentiality means?

R: Yes.

Dr: Can you tell me what it means?

R: I tell you private things and you pretend not to tell my parents.

Dr: Let's not get off on the wrong foot. I want you to trust me.

R: Ok.

Dr: What's your favourite colour?

R: Blue.

Dr: What a coincidence. Mine too. My eyes are blue. Are yours?

R: No. My eyes are green.

Dr: Do you like to watch television?

R: Sometimes.

Dr: What do you like to watch?

R: Most recently I've been watching coverage about the people killed in Greensboro, North Carolina at the Death to the Klan rally but that's sort of been pushed aside because of this Iran hostage thing.

Dr: That's no fun for a little girl to watch.

R: I imagine it's less fun for the hostages.

Dr: What about cartoons? Do you ever watch cartoons?

R: Sometimes.

Dr: What's your favourite?

R: Looney Tunes. Bugs Bunny, not Road Runner. I hate that the Coyote never catches the Road Runner. Other than that, maybe… The Jetsons and Flintstones.

Dr: I have a niece right around your age and her favourite movies are Cinderella and Snow White. Have you seen them?

R: Yes.

Dr: What did you think?

R: I didn't like Cinderella but Snow White was ok.

Dr: Why didn't you like Cinderella?

R: It wasn't very believable.

Dr: And The Jetsons and Flintstones are?

R: Those shows aren't believable in a different way.

Dr: Do you ever wet the bed?

R: What's that got to do with cartoons?

Dr: Nothing. We're moving on. When was the last time you wet the bed?

R: I had an accident back in the summer but I'd been eating lots of watermelon and I dreamed that I was already in the bathroom. So it really doesn't count.

Dr: Do you ever have bad dreams?

R: Does this count?

Dr: Rachel, one of the reasons you're here is that your mother is concerned by some of the things your sister has confided. She has expressed worry that you are sexually active. Don't you think that ten is entirely too young for sexual experimentation?

R: I've already told everybody that Julie was lying.

Dr: Well, for the sake of this discussion, let's pretend that Julie wasn't lying.

R: I don't want to pretend that Julie wasn't lying.

Dr: It is important for you to be honest with me, Rachel.

R: Do you want me to be honest or do you want me to pretend that Julie's lies are true?

Dr: Why would Julie lie about something like this?

R: Julie lies even if the truth sounds better.

Dr: Rachel, I don't want you to try to be so grown up. There's no need for argumentative tactics. The world upon which you are teetering is fraught with complex emotions, emotions that you aren't equipped to deal with yet. You should focus on activities that allow you to access your inner child. A day at the park. Colouring books, sketch pads, perhaps a book of stickers. Dance or gymnastics. You should think happy thoughts and try not to be afraid of the child within.

R: But I *am* a child.

Dr: Yes dear but you're not very childlike.

Leaving is my colour.

While my father was having lawn fertilizer pumped from his stomach, I sat in the waiting room with Frank.

Julie was in Helsinki at the Baltic Herring Food Festival with nineteen of her closest see-you-once-a-year sorority sisters. Mother was at home in hysterics.

I said, 'Thanks for coming.'

Frank said, 'No problem. I'm sure he'll be fine.' He offered me a stick of gum. 'Julie was upset that she couldn't be here.'

'It's probably best she isn't.'

'You know, she needs you more than she lets on.'

'I know. She needs me to be her own personal whipping post and scapegoat.'

'That's not exactly true.'

'Perhaps not so much now that she has you.'

I walked over to the vending machines and tried to get a coffee. The machine took all my change except one nickel that it kept spitting out. Frank stepped up close beside me and opened a palm full of change. I took a nickel. It worked.

I said, 'It's nice of you to be concerned but there is so much history that you don't know and I'm sure you've only heard one side of the story. Julie can be cruel.'

'And you?'

The doctor opened the emergency room doors and said, 'Bennett?'

'That's me.'

'Mister Bennett is out of immediate danger but we're moving him upstairs to a private suite.'

'Can I see him?'

'Not yet. If you'll just bear with us a moment longer you can go in. The hospital publicist is with him now.'

'Publicist?'

'Your father is extremely generous with the hospital and opportunities such as this are usually… documented.'

'So, basically, he's signing autographs?'

'Something like that.'

★ ★ ★

When I left the cottage I wasn't sure where I was going.

The Volvo in front of me had a New York license plate.

The city that never sleeps sounded good to me.

I had been on the road for a couple of hours when my father called. I put him on speaker phone and asked, 'Have you been injured in an automobile or on-the-job accident through no fault of your own?'

He laughed. 'Very funny. So, that didn't last long.'

'What did you expect? It was like swimming with piranhas.'

'Talk to me, Rachel.'

'I am talking to you.'

'You're not thinking clearly, running out like that was the last thing you needed to do. All of this has been very disconcerting I know but now is a time to listen to the people who love you.'

'Where are you?'

'Los Angeles.'

'I want to see you, not Mother or Julie. Can you come here?'

'Of course I can. I've got meetings all day tomorrow and a business dinner Wednesday. I'll be in San Francisco Thursday. If you turn around and go straight back to the cottage I can be there by Friday. No later than Saturday evening.'

'Forget it.'

'No, don't be like that. I'll be there as soon as I can.'

'Don't bother.'

'I wish you'd let us help you.'

'I'll help myself.'

'See where that's got you. Do you even know where you're

going?'

'New York.'

'That's the first sensible thing I've heard you say. Will you do as you're told for once in your life and go see Wallace as soon as you get there? I'll call him now and tell him you're on the way.'

'Ok.'

'Did you have sense enough to take the credit cards with you?'

'I did.'

'Cash?'

'No.'

'I'll make sure Wallace has something for you then. Stay in New York a few weeks, darling. And don't make any rash decisions until we've had a chance to talk.'

★ ★ ★

I met Wallace for the first time when I was twelve.

He took care of us while they finished building our house during our 'holding pattern visit' to New York (as my father sometimes called it). Mother ran Wallace ragged, back and forth to design shops for fabric and carpet samples as she decorated from a distance.

The first time we came to New York it took some getting used to.

Living fifty storeys up was much different than living in a single-level house in Alabama.

Even Julie was happy.

She sat on the bathroom counter eating pistachio nuts while I took a bubble bath. She was laughing and tossing shells into the water with me.

It was lonesome being away from Phillip and Jack but there were plenty of distractions:

1. Simon and Garfunkel in Central Park.
2. Camelot on Broadway.

3. Trifecta: Empire State Building, World Trade Center, Statue of Liberty.
4. Panic in Grand Central Station.
5. Metropolitan Museum of Art.
6. Thanksgiving at Tavern on the Green.
7. Christmas tree lighting at Rockefeller Center.

But the thing I remember best was: Mother and Julie had the flu.

On my thirteenth birthday Mother and Julie were too sick to get out of bed and they had to stay at home while I went on an after-hours shopping spree at FAO Schwartz with my father, Miles and Gloria.

That night I ate pink marshmallows and watched *Barney Miller* on television while my father read the paper. I fell asleep happy.

★ ★ ★

Wallace was waiting for me when I arrived. He was apologetic that the Ty Warner wasn't available. The best he could do was fifty-one floors up. The Presidential Suite.

It made me laugh.

The Four Seasons is a nice place.

Wallace said, 'We've only managed to stock the refrigerator with a few of the items your father requested, but I promise as soon as you are rested, we shall stock the balance of your requirements.'

'Please don't trouble yourself, really. I don't have any *requirements*. I don't even know how long I'll be here.'

'It is no trouble, Miss Bennett. Have your bags been accounted for?'

'I don't have much luggage.'

He looked at my grey sweat pants and tried to smile, 'Well then, tomorrow we must do something about that as well. Rest now. Joseph will show you to your suite.'

'I don't like all this fuss, Wallace. How lost can a person get in an elevator?'

'You'd be surprised.'

* * *

I made conversation with Joseph on the elevator ride up.

He was an actor. Graduated from Juilliard.

He had an audition the next day for a part on *CSI: New York* and although he hadn't been in a production of any great importance he said that he had once delivered a singing telegram to Nathan Lane.

I was a Nathan Lane fan. I was impressed.

Joseph said, 'Everything went fine at the start but then one of his bodyguards got me in a full nelson.'

I wished him luck and assured him there was no need for him to escort me all the way to my room.

* * *

Mother called the next morning.

She was mad.

'Where are you?'

The way she said it gave me a momentary fright, as if maybe she was in the lobby of the hotel, so I asked, 'Where are you?'

'I'm where I'm supposed to be.'

'That sounds very Zen.'

'You could have had the common courtesy to tell me you were leaving.'

'Why? You didn't tell me you were arriving.'

'This is my house and I'll come and go as I please.'

'That's my father's house.'

'You could have told me you were leaving before I went through the trouble of planning a nice meal. Now I'm stuck with all this fresh crab meat.'

'I think the neighbour has a dog.'

Mother hung up.

I could hear somebody trying to call while Mother was on the line but they were gone by the time I answered. It took a moment for voicemail to come through and, from the brevity of the message, I wondered how many attempts she'd made.

It was Julie.

She said, 'Phillip knows you're in town. He's expecting you for lunch at one p.m.'

I didn't want to think.

I crawled back into bed and went to sleep.

★ ★ ★

I don't know how long I was asleep but I woke up to a flurry of knocks at the door.

I ignored them.

The door opened and Wallace said, 'Hello? Miss Bennett?'

'Give me a second Wallace, I'm still in bed.'

'No hurry. We'll get things ready for you.'

Wallace had enough staff with him to make up a hockey squad. Some were armed with groceries. Some were carrying gift bags from the spa. Some were wheeling racks of clothes.

Wallace said, 'All right, let's see what we can do about this fashion crisis.'

I made gentle objections as I watched them stocking the refrigerator and picking up my dirty panties from the bathroom floor. One of them was trying to brush my hair while two others were wrapping measuring tapes around my breasts and waist.

When one of the women introduced herself as Nadia and started to pull my shirt over my head I felt something in my brain pop.

I asked them to leave.

I said, 'Wallace, none of this is necessary.'

'But your father said…'

'Never mind what my father said, please just get out. I can't deal with this right now.'

'I have one special request from your father. I'll leave it here for you.'

I opened the bag and it was a cantaloupe-coloured scarf.

I held it to my face and breathed in deeply but it smelled of nothing familiar, just chemicals and dyes. I threw it across the room and went back to bed.

★ ★ ★

When my father stayed away on especially long business trips he always returned bearing gifts. On one such occasion, Mother got a bottle of Chanel No. 5. I got a cantaloupe-coloured cashmere sweater that he saw in the window of a vintage clothing store and when I put it on he raved about how pretty I looked. It smelled like freshly cut grass.

He looked at Julie and asked, 'What's wrong Jules? Don't you like your teddy bear?'

'Yes, it's fine.'

My father held the bear up and wriggled its head. 'Come on little girl, I've travelled a long way to be your friend,' my father said for the bear.

Julie said, 'It came from the airport.'

'No it didn't.'

'Ok then, the bag and receipt came from the airport.'

She went back to solving her Rubik's cube.

Written in the stars.

Mother accepts full responsibility for the tension in our relationship. She told me so one afternoon as she picked through a chicken Caesar salad.

She said, 'It's my fault. I shouldn't have had sex with your father in February.'

I should have kept quiet but I didn't. 'What are you talking about?'

'I realize now that this block between us is a fundamental incompatibility of signs.'

'Signs?'

'Signs. Yes, our zodiac signs. I'm a Libra and should have never had a Scorpio child. Especially not one with Sun in Scorpio and Moon in Cancer with an ascendant Libra! I've been consulting with the most brilliant astrologist and she says that, according to our birth charts, there is little to no chance of us ever enjoying a stable relationship.'

'You needed to pay an astrologist to tell you that? Astrology is a crock.'

'She was right, see. She supposed you would have that type of reaction. Your sun makes you defiant and suspicious and your moon makes you resistant to new ideas and far too sensitive for constructive criticism. Rachel, your Mars is in Capricorn! It's in Capricorn! Honey, that makes you hard and bitter and vindictive!'

'Can I have your croutons?'

'My sun is in Libra with a Pisces moon and an ascendant Scorpio. I mean, it's just a wonder we haven't killed each other yet. I'm imaginative and quick-witted. I have the ability to think logically with compassion and forgiveness. I mean, honey, my Uranus is in Libra, for heaven's sake. Do you know what that means?'

'Does it mean that you're going to give me your croutons?'

Mother signalled to the waiter to bring the check.

★ ★ ★

I once asked Mother, 'Why don't I have chores?'

She said, 'Because we have Minnie for that sort of thing.'

I said, 'But chores are character building.'

'Who in the world told you *that*?'

'Darla Jones. She's got chores and her mother says that chores are character building and that I'll grow up to have bad character because I don't have any chores.'

'Well, Darla Jones' mother wears white after Labor Day. What does she know?'

'Isn't there something I could do around here?'

'I don't know. What skills do you have?'

'I'm not sure.'

'With an attitude like that, you'll never get hired at an interview. Be confident and assertive.'

'Ok then. I want some chores… *now*!'

'Here, Rachel, move over. My show is back on.'

I didn't move.

'I can't see the television.'

I didn't move.

'I don't care what chores you do, just move out of the way. Go ask Minnie, she'll give you something to do.'

I asked Minnie and she gave me something to do. I folded a whole dryer load of bath towels all by myself. Later I saw Mother throwing all of the towels out of the linen closet because they were folded wrong. They weren't even. None of the corners symmetrically matched and they were folded short side to short side rather than long to long.

Nobody told me the job required a ruler and a level. I never asked to fold towels again.

Therapy: A One-Act Play.

Characters:
Dr Michelle Vickarman (Dr): Psychiatrist. Slightly feral, rat-like in appearance.
Rachel (R): Patient. Slightly off-put.

Dr: This way. I have a new office.

R: I've never been down this way before.

Dr: No, you wouldn't have been. Here we are. Just have a seat please.

R: It's bigger. Better view too.

Dr: Yes. I am going to repaint and get rid of the horse motif.

R: Horses are nice.

Dr: They're not really me. Candy?

R: No thanks.

Dr: They're strawberry. Are you sure?

R: I'm sure.

Dr: Let's get started then. Last time we discussed different approaches to therapy. I suggested an eclectic mix, something including but not limited to cognitive behaviour and psychodynamic therapy, along with a prescribed course of medication. Tell me, what do you hope to get out of therapy?

R: I'm not sure.

Dr: Let's think about it for a moment because if you don't know what you'd like to get out of therapy then our sessions will be less than productive.

R: Do you have a menu or something I can choose from?

Dr: Do you often approach uncomfortable situations with humour?

R: I try not to approach uncomfortable situations.

Dr: Interesting. Life is full of uncomfortable situations. Don't you find it difficult to avoid uncomfortable situations?

R: I didn't say I managed to avoid uncomfortable situations but I try not to approach them.

Dr: So, you're basing the joke about uncomfortable situations on semantics. Do you enjoy being clever?

R: I'm sorry. I was distracted, trying to count how many times we've said 'uncomfortable situations'. What was the question again? Did it happen to have anything to do with uncomfortable situations?

Dr: How are the obsessive thoughts?

R: They're fine.

Dr: And the self-harm?

R: It's fine too.

Dr: Could you explain in greater detail what you mean by 'fine'?

R: I'm sorry I don't understand the question.

Dr: How often do you experience obsessive thoughts?

R: Do you mean how many times a day?

Dr: In general.

R: I'm not sure. Say for instance I don't sleep for 24 hours because I can't stop daydreaming about being beaten with a lead pipe. Do I count that as one instance or do I count it as several?

Dr: Are you having trouble sleeping?

R: Yes.

Dr: I can prescribe something for that. What about the self-harm?

R: What about it?

Dr: Have you hurt yourself lately?

R: Yes.

Dr: In an extreme way?

R: Yes.

Dr: Did you require medical attention?

R: Yes.

Dr: And how did you feel afterwards?

R: After the self-harm or the medical treatment?

Dr: Both.

R: Fine.

Dr: Are you taking your medication?

R: Yes.

Dr: Did you have an opportunity to read the pamphlet I sent home with you last time?

R: Yes.

Dr: Did you find it helpful?

R: 'Helpful' is such a relative word.

Dr: Did you do the exercises suggested in the pamphlet?

R: Yes.

Dr: Did you bring them with you?

R: Yes.

Dr: Great. I'm very pleased. Shall we have a look at them?

R: Ok.

Dr: Great. So, the first questions is: what time of day do you find the obsessive thoughts to be the most prevalent?

R: All day.

Dr: Did you notice a peak in the thoughts at any particular time of the day?

R: Not really. I seemed consistently fixated and experienced no peaks, no valleys.

Dr: When you experienced the obsessive thoughts, what positive steps did you take to alleviate the situation?

R: Again, 'positive' is relative.

Dr: Not really.

R: Well, sort of.

Dr: Did you engage in any of the activities I suggested for when these obsessive thoughts become a problem? Did you try colouring? Drawing? Giving your inner child a chance to relax and perhaps even use that inner child to calm the warring grown-up?

R: No, I didn't try that.

Dr: What did you do in response to these obsessive thoughts?

R: I'm sorry. Distracted again. I was trying to count 'obsessives'.

Dr: When you find yourself gripped by these obsessive thoughts, how did you answer the feelings?

R: Is that a trick question?

Dr: No.

R: It's just that… you asked me how I answered. If I say… I answered 'blah', fill in the blank, then you'll come back with something like: when you say *answered* does that mean you're hearing voices?

Dr: It's not a trick question. What did you do in response to these obsessive thoughts?

R: We've got to be nearing ten obsessives by now. But to answer your question, I either binged or cut myself.

Dr: Before you cut, did you consider my suggestion about drawing on yourself with a red marker instead?

R: I can't say that I gave that serious consideration.

Dr: Just to go back for a moment, are you hearing voices?

R: Just yours.

Dr: How are you responding to the medications?

R: We aren't on speaking terms yet.

Dr: What does that mean?

R: Nothing.

Dr: Are you taking the medications as prescribed?

R: Yes.

Dr: I suggest we increase to forty milligrams and I have another prescription I'd like to add. It is typically used in cessation treatment but there are promising studies as regards obsessive compulsive disorder as well. You might experience side effects but they should dissipate.

R: What kind of side effects?

Dr: Nose bleeds, headaches, dizziness, numbness in your extremities, unexpected anal leakage.

R: Is there any other kind?

Dr: Pardon me?

R: Never mind.

Dr: Any suicidal ideation?

R: That sounds exotic.

Dr: Any thoughts of killing yourself?

R: No more than usual.

Dr: Do you consider yourself a threat?

R: I don't like to flatter myself.

Dr: Rachel, let's be clear here, ok? I have an obligation to pass my findings on to my supervisors and the mental health advisory should I deem you a threat to yourself or others. Please answer the question. Are you suicidal?

R: If I say yes, then you have the authority to impose involuntary treatment?

Dr: Yes.

R: Then, no.

Dr: Do you plan on harming anybody else?

R: No.

Dr: Ok, here are the two new prescriptions.

R: Thanks.

Dr: Oh, wait. I forgot the sleeping pills.

R: Don't forget those.

Dr: Take one before bedtime when you are certain that you can dedicate at least eight hours to sleep.

R: That's quite a commitment. Most of my relationships don't last that long.

Dr: I'd like to give you more reading material. Would you like the pamphlet on body dysmorphic disorder or bipolar disorder?

R: Let's go crazy, give me both. Sorry, no pun intended.

Dr: See the receptionist out front to make another appointment in two weeks.

R: I need to hurry this along, if you don't mind. My insurance is no good after the 31st.

Dr: Ok, tell her to work you in twice next week.

R: I never really know how to say goodbye to you. Should I hug you or shake your hand or just say thank you?

Dr: I have another patient waiting. We can discuss your exit issues next time.

Raising the dead.

Julie's message said that Phillip was expecting me for lunch but I couldn't make myself get out of bed.

I showed up late and even then, I stood outside his studio for a long time trying to decide whether or not I wanted to see him.

That alone should have been a clear sign. Phillip had always been good to me and good for me.

I was just about to leave when I realized that he was standing right beside me eating a sandwich.

He said, 'I was starving. I couldn't wait any longer.'

I said, 'Is that a ham sandwich? Your mother would have a conniption.'

'It wouldn't be her first.' He finished what was left of his lunch in two bites. I watched him chew. He watched me watching. We didn't smile or laugh. We just stood there in a matter-of-fact way until he wadded the wrapper up and put it in his pocket. Then he grabbed me up close to him and kissed me on the cheek. 'You Babysnake! How the hell are you?'

'I'm fine.'

'You're not fine. Come on, I'm spitting feathers. Let's find something to drink.'

★ ★ ★

We went into Phillip's shop.

He said, 'Shichi, will you bring me some tea please?'

Shichi asked, 'What kind of tea would you like?'

'The Broken Orange stuff.'

'Pekoe.' Shichi looked at me and asked, 'Will you have some too?'

I said, 'No thanks.'

She said, 'I bring it. If you don't want it. Fine. If you do want it. Fine.'

The shop was a provocative departure from the expected. It was luxurious and tactile. All of the senses were tempted, but it had an irresistible edge, something appealingly off-kilter. It was like waking from a deep sleep with the dream reel still playing and you aren't quite sure if it's ecstasy or nightmare.

I fell in love with the shop.

Phillip said, 'You like it. I can tell.'

'I do.'

'Good.'

I said, 'How in the world do you afford this place?'

'Have you seen the price tags?'

'I'm serious. Prime location, massive floor space. How did you get the money to do it?'

'Like you don't know.'

'I don't know.'

'Your father was my first investor. I assumed you put him up to it.'

'No.'

'He put me in touch with a woman named Abby Linarez from Belize and things took off. We've got the restaurant over there, can you smell that soup? It's this vegetarian thing they make. Shichi won't tell me what she puts in it, says I wouldn't touch it again. You know how I am. They do facials and massages upstairs. You should get one while you're here.'

'I had no idea. I'm glad he helped you. But I had no idea.'

I picked up a wooden bucket from the shelf and looked at it. I turned it over, looked at the price tag and said, 'Does this have one too many zeros?'

Phillip laughed. 'I told you. They're antique Chinese rice buckets and no kidding, they cost me about a tenth of what that price tag says. It's robbery of the worst kind. But people can't get enough of it. The more I charge the more they want it. Come over here and have a look at this. Have you ever seen a Black Orchid? These orchids are…'

Mid-sentence Phillip grabbed my shoulders and used me as a shield. He said, 'Oh God Abraham Moses Mother, please I am sorry. Pork shall never pass my lips again, please don't let her see me.'

'What are you talking about?'

I turned around to see and he grabbed me again. 'Don't look at it!'

A woman behind me said, 'Phillip? Phillip is that you darling?'

His shoulders sank. He whispered, 'I deserve this.'

He put on a succulent smile. In a voice all sugar crystals and peppermint sticks he said, 'Olivia Brandt Merriwinkle, you divine creature, to what do I owe the pleasure?'

She kissed him, twice: either cheek. 'It's a matter of great discretion. May we speak in private?'

'Speak freely. I assure you that your confidence is safe with Rachel. She's my Raleigh Philpot.'

Olivia looked at me with admiration and said, 'Pleasure, I'm sure.'

I said, 'Likewise.'

Shichi brought the tea. We sat down in a relatively secluded area of the store, next to a slate wall covered with a constant sheet of falling water. I tried to ask Phillip who the hell Raleigh Philpot was but he gave me a horrified look and whispered, 'Later!'

Phillip said, 'Olivia, you were saying?'

'I need something spectacular. It's for a Davies-Wharton.'

'Leila or Madeline?'

'Discretion, darling, remember discretion.' She whispered, 'It's for Madeline. She's had a *procedure*.'

'A *procedure*, I see. Terribly involved?'

'New chin. But she doesn't want anybody to know.'

I said, 'Phillip, if you don't mind? Missus Merriwinkle, I understand the gravity of your situation. It is certainly a delicate matter and requires a special arrangement. I suggest you allow Phillip to create a living work of art cradled in a piece of history itself: an antique Chinese rice bucket.'

Olivia collected her purse and stood up. 'I'll take two of the Chinese buckets.' She looked at me and said, 'Are you free for dinner this evening? I could use someone like you on my team.'

I said, 'I'm sorry, Missus Merriwinkle. It will have to wait until my next visit to New York. Matters of delicacy. You'll understand.'

'Of course I do. Yes. Until then.' She held her hand out to Phillip. He kissed it. 'I knew I could count on you.'

'Yes, Olivia. Always, darling.'

★ ★ ★

As soon as we ordered dinner I asked, 'Who is Raleigh Philpot?'

Phillip looked around. He said, 'Not so loud. That name still raises a bristle.'

A waiter stopped at our table and delivered two drinks.

Phillip said, 'This isn't what we ordered.'

'Two Green Apple Martinis compliments of the woman at the end of the bar.'

Phillip turned to look. An older woman waved and blew him a kiss.

I asked, 'Is she wearing jodhpurs?'

Phillip turned back around and started folding and refolding his napkin. He said, 'Probably.'

'I think she's got a riding crop. Why would she bring a riding crop to dinner?'

'I'm pretty sure it's a prop for later.'

'Oh.'

'Try not to think about it. It'll put you off your food.'

I whispered, 'Raleigh Philpot.'

The waiter brought our drinks and Phillip said, 'Would you please take these green things away. Anybody who would put schnapps in a martini should be shot.'

Phillip pointed at his glass and said, 'Take this now. This is a real drink. Yoichi, twenty year. Japanese. People make fun, sure. Nobody can get past Highland Whisky and I'll give due, Highland Whisky is brilliant but this… this is a work of art. A masterpiece.' He took a drink. 'It takes *days* to finish.'

I felt very ordinary sipping my Grey Goose.

We sat in silence for a while. Phillip revelling in his single malt, me trying not to make eye contact with the galloping granny at the bar.

Phillip finally said, 'If I tell you about Raleigh Philpot, I have to tell you about the Tesse-Givneys first. Kara Tesse and Christian Givney. They met in college. There has never been, in the history of all mismatched couples, a *more* mismatched couple. Kara looked like an irresistible vision of death. 'Pale' comes nowhere close to describing this woman's skin. She was flawlessly white. And where she might have been redeemed by a shock of jet black hair, no, her hair was the colour of oatmeal. A monochromatic vixen with legs for days. She was tall. Taller than me. I bet she was six foot one in her stocking feet.'

Our appetizers arrived.

I said, 'This looks delicious.'

Phillip said, 'Yeah, does. What did you get?'

'Duck with pear and Sambuca.'

'I got liver.'

'Do you want to swap?'

He said, 'Sure, if you want to. I don't know why I ordered liver. I hate liver.'

'You're pitiful. Give it here.'

He said, 'Anyway, Christian was about as exciting as sliced bread. He was short and dark and stubbly. The man had a five o'clock shadow by nine a.m. He always wore a cheap navy blue suit. When they went out together it looked like the postman out for a stroll with an exotic animal. The only thing they had in common was: they both came from ultra-rich families. No offence but it wouldn't have broken their little pink piggy bank to buy and sell your father three times over.'

'We're not talking about my father.'

'I'm just saying. These two came from generations of bankers. I'm pretty sure they used the term 'banker' loosely in the beginning, maybe even interchangeable with criminal, gangster. Running liquor with the Kennedys for fun. That kind of thing. When they got married it was like warring nations aligning. Brokers around the world gave a sigh of relief. The Tesse-Givneys were finally in bed together, literally. Kara and Christian started off small. The families brought them in as corporate financiers. Mergers. Acquisitions. But they didn't stay small for long. Those two were money magnets.'

I said, 'How does Raleigh Philpot fit into all of this?'

'I'm getting to that. Raleigh Philpot was, technically, their butler. I knew him. He was a round-faced, unassuming fellow. Very well spoken. Very polite. Dry sense of humour. He did everything for them. So when Kara got bored with the money-making game, which is understandable, they had enough money to last ten lifetimes, she decided that she wanted to explore the softer side of womanhood. Kara wanted a baby.'

'Don't tell me Raleigh provided the genetic material.'

'No, he did better. He provided the whole baby. Kara wasn't interested in going through the whole nine months of a big belly thing and she certainly wasn't interested in going through labour. She was a Tesse-Givney! Be reasonable.'

'So Raleigh stole a baby for her?'

'Would you let me tell the story?'

The waiter cleared the appetizer plates and served the main course. As soon as he was out of earshot I told Phillip to stop eyeing my veal. He said he was happy with his tartar.

'How did Raleigh get a baby for them?'

'It isn't unheard of. He just made some... arrangements. It wasn't illegal. Not really. It was a boy. Not an infant but young enough that they felt certain they could get the 'common' stink off him. Kara and Christian were proud parents. They named him Sebastian Romanoff Tesse-Givney.'

'Why do rich people and celebrities always name their kids something strange?'

'I've no idea. Next time you see that waiter, stop him. I need another drink.'

'Ok.'

'I think their fascination with parenthood lasted about as long as the remodel did. They bought the condo below their penthouse so that little Sebastian would have a whole 'wing' to himself. By the time the wing was finished Kara had had enough of Sebastian spitting up on her Prada blouses. She ordered Christian to prepare the yacht and they left for an indefinite trip around the world. Raleigh was left with as much money as he needed and a baby to look after.'

'And that's it?'

'Like that isn't enough! But no ma'am that's not "it". Can I have a bite of that please?'

'I didn't think you liked veal?'

'I didn't either.'

I cut a piece and put it on his plate. He looked at me expectantly.

I said, 'You want some of the asparagus too?'

'Yes please.'

'You never cease to amaze me. Why don't you let me order dessert for you so you won't try to take mine away?'

'What would be the fun in that? Anyway, Sebastian grew up just fine. He had all the luxuries of a baby Tesse-Givney. Private clubs. Private schools. Private parties. He saw mommy and daddy on Christmas and Easter, who could ask for more, right? He was a very handsome boy. It looked like Raleigh spit-shined him every morning before he went off to school. Meanwhile back at the farm, things weren't going so well with the family store. The market wasn't what it used to be and as more and more doom and gloom hit the headlines certain rumours started surfacing of gross misconduct on none other than Christian Givney's part. Seems Christian and Kara had made a few overzealous promises to investors and not only were they losing returns, they were losing their asses. So they came back to New York to minimize the damage and see if they couldn't quell some of the fears. And while they were back, Christian decided to spend some time with Sebastian.'

Phillip leaned in close and whispered the rest. He said, 'The story goes that Raleigh caught Christian performing acts of an unspeakable nature on Sebastian. Raleigh took Christian into the bathroom and bludgeoned him to death with a marble door stop. Kara came in during the middle of the scuffle. She didn't want to be rude, apparently, so she allowed Raleigh to finish. She told him to go downstairs and her driver would take him to the police station. Which Raleigh did. He made a full confession and wonder of all wonders, Kara's attorney got him off with six years' probation.'

'What happened to Sebastian?'

'Last I heard he'd moved to Spain and was working in a library shelving books.'

'What happened to Raleigh?'

'If he isn't dead by now, he's in Spain taking care of Sebastian.'

* * *

After dinner, Phillip and I went back to his place for a nightcap. When we got there a woman was asleep with her back resting against Phillip's door.

Phillip said, 'This isn't going to be pretty.'

He touched her on the shoulder and said, 'Lilly.'

Lilly looked up and practically threw herself into his arms. Phillip hugged her for a moment and then asked, 'How did you get in here?'

'Well, it's good to see you too! Is that any way to say hello?'

Then Lilly saw me. She said, 'Do *not* tell me that this is the reason you needed a break?'

Phillip gave me his keys and said, 'I'll meet you inside.'

I said, 'I better go.'

'Go inside.'

He stayed in the hall talking to Lilly for a long time. When he came back in he explained that Lilly had lived with him for a while but that things hadn't gone well. When he asked her to move out she went berserk and threatened to kill herself. He opened a drawer and pointed to the gun and said, 'I have no idea where she got it and I have no idea what to do with it.'

Phillip went to make drinks and I took the gun from the drawer. It was much heavier than I expected. I put the gun to my head and rested the muzzle against my temple. I heard glass breaking behind me. Phillip slapped the gun out of my hand and pulled me down to the floor.

'What the fuck are you doing?'

'I was only seeing what it felt like. I wasn't going to do it.'

'How was I supposed to know that? Oh, you bitch. You bitch.' Phillip couldn't catch his breath.

'Calm down or you'll hyperventilate.'

'I am hyperventilating. What did you expect?' He was starting to scare me. He was gasping frantically and I could hardly understand what he was saying. He kept pointing to the other room. 'Get the tank. The tank. Go in there, there… in there and get the oxygen tank.' I wheeled it in to him and he put the mask on. I curled up next to him on the floor and within a few minutes he was fine.

'Why do you have an oxygen tank?'

'You wouldn't believe me if I told you.'

'I might.'

'It's a long story and involves sex with what some might term a "mature" woman. Think: Green Apple Martinis and a riding crop. Beyond that, you don't want to know. And don't change the subject.'

'Did we have a subject?'

'I absolutely cannot believe you would do that to me. I can't believe you would want me to see you like that. You have no idea how much you mean to me.'

I laughed. 'I see. You aren't concerned with what I might have been feeling if I *was* serious about pulling the trigger. Just miffed that I would do it in your house.'

'Exactly!'

When we were together, Phillip and I were always able to find a necessary path from profound sorrow and heartbreak to humour verging on the perverse.

He said, 'Madam, do you have any idea how long it would have taken me to wash you out of this white shag carpet?'

★ ★ ★

The next morning when I woke up, Phillip was looking at me.

He said, 'I love you dearly but there's no civilized sleeping with you.'

'What do you mean?'

'You kick like a mule and snore like you've got a poodle lodged in your sinus cavity.'

'I do not.'

'But you do.'

I sat up and looked out the window. I said, 'Is it snowing?'

Phillip said, 'It sho' am. Tell me you've got a warmer coat than what you had on last night.'

'Have you got to work today?'

Phillip was putting on his socks. He said, 'I do. But it's early. Go back to sleep for a while then meet me at the shop for lunch. Shichi'll give you some of that mystery soup.'

'I think I'm going to head out today.'

'Don't do that, stay for a while. Stay with me.'

'I need to go down to Birmingham and check on my things.'

'What "things"?'

'They put all my stuff in storage when I went to rehab and I need to make sure everything's all right.'

'Why wouldn't it be all right? Come on, there's no rush for that. Anyway, what have you got down there that you couldn't replace by this afternoon?'

'My grandmother's spoons.'

'What do you care about a bunch of old spoons?'

'She gave them to me. It was a big deal. She didn't really do "gifts". Mother was so jealous I thought she was going to jump through her own asshole.'

'Oh, spare me. I swear sometimes you can be a royal barbarian. Your mother's not *that* bad. Sometimes mothers *are* human, you know.'

'Yes, and sometimes they eat their young.'

'Have somebody from your father's office get the spoons. You stay here with me.'

'I'll probably go visit Jack while I'm there.'

'And the shoe drops. You should try the truth more often, it suits you.'

'I'm not lying. There's nothing covert about it. I'm going to Birmingham. Jack lives in Birmingham. What's wrong with me saying hello while I'm down there? I'm in New York. I came to see you. What's the difference?'

'I wish there wasn't a difference. But there is. Just take it easy for a while. Don't make that trip yet.'

'Why not?'

Phillip was quiet for a moment. He reached over and gently pinched my earlobe. 'Promise me you won't go.'

'I have to. I still love him.'

'Things change, Babysnake.'

'Real love lasts forever.'

'I'm afraid forever isn't as long as you think.'

Lie Down with Dogs, Get Up with Me.

Sometime just before I was arrested and just after I started blacking out I acquired a pet.

I woke up on my laundry room floor, fully dressed but soaking wet.

It was morning, although I wasn't sure which morning.

The tub was still full of water. Apparently I'd taken a bath with my clothes on. The water was extremely muddy. I couldn't account for the mud but it wasn't necessarily a surprise.

I took my clothes off and got into bed.

I hadn't been in bed long when I felt something on the bed with me.

It felt big. I didn't open my eyes, hoping that if it was a giant rat it might get bored and wander away. It didn't.

When I opened my eyes there was a droopy-jowled, curly-headed Springer Spaniel looking at me. He was wet too.

I said, 'I hope you bought me dinner first.' At which point he licked me on the forehead and wallowed around on the bed trying to dry off.

I got up and found some dry clothes so I could take the rascal for a walk. Once outside, it was obvious I was in the company of a fugitive. It looked like a ticker tape parade. Flyers posted everywhere offering a reward for the return of a Springer Spaniel named Baxter. The people at 1414 Kinder Drive wanted this dog back in a bad way.

We started walking in that direction.

When we got close to the house three screaming kids came running out of the garage. The mother followed. Baxter seemed glad to see them.

One of the kids said, 'Yuck, he's all wet.'

It wasn't raining.

The mother shook my hand and said, 'Thank you. Thank you. Oh, Baxter, get down you brat, don't jump. Get down.' Baxter was glad to see her too. She said, 'Thank you so much for finding him, the kids were beside themselves. Somebody broke into our backyard, took Baxter, a twenty-pound bag of dog food, his leash, all his toys. They must have been planning to keep him. We have a tiny teacup poodle too that stays in the house and this morning when we let her out for a wee, she must have gone out looking for Baxter and right out the open gate because now we've lost her too.'

I said, 'Well, this was the only one in the house with me this morning.'

She said, 'In the house?'

'At the house. Outside the house.'

She looked at me. She said, 'Why is he wet?'

'I've no idea.'

'Your hair is wet.'

'It is.'

She said, 'What did you say your name was?'

'I didn't.'

'Hold on just a minute, let me get my husband.'

I ran.

When I got home I found these things in the kitchen: a bag of dog food, a leash and a slobber-covered tennis ball.

The Path of the Righteous.

I waited for Phillip to go to work before I left.

It seemed easier that way.

I went back to the hotel and packed the food and toiletries Wallace *et entourage* had left that morning.

I packed the clothes that were still hanging on racks in front of the television. I wasn't sure if I'd have occasion to wear the Valentino couture. I packed it anyway. The accompanying hat was too big to fit into my bag.

I phoned the front desk and asked them to have my car ready. Wallace was waiting for me.

'Miss Bennett, there's someone here to see you.'

'To see *me*?'

'If you'll come this way.'

Wallace took me alongside the front desk and down a long corridor that I'd never noticed before. He opened the last door on the right and showed me into a lavishly decorated office.

It was Miles.

'Come in. Come in. Have a seat.' Miles motioned for me to sit down and said, 'There's a chill in the room, Wallace.'

'I'll see to it, sir.' He closed the door as he left.

I said, 'Is this your home away from home?'

Miles said, 'I feel at home wherever I go.'

'I was just on my way out.'

'So I hear. Let's keep this short and sweet then, shall we?' He sat down in the chair across from me.

I said, 'I'm curious what brings you here, no coincidence I'm sure.'

'What do you hope to accomplish with all this childish behaviour?'

'I don't know what you're talking about.'

'Perhaps that is part of the problem. Let's define terms. By childish behaviour I simply mean, swallowing pills, attempting suicide, shirking rehabilitation, not to mention complete disregard for your mother and father.'

'Since when are you concerned about my mother?'

'On the contrary, I've spent much of the last thirty years concerned about the well-being of your mother. My happiness has come at a price.'

'You've been screwing my father for the last thirty years is another way to say it.'

'What a coarse little rat you can be. It must please you to be slightly more clever than most. No doubt you take pleasure in administering this shoot-from-the-hip attitude. Effective in disarming the everyman, isn't it? For the most part, though, I find your acerbic wit a rather thin veil. My opinion?'

'Do I have a choice?'

'You're a spoiled woman-child who refuses to grow up because she has a twenty-four-karat-gold security net. I hope some day you endeavour to deserve your father's kindness.'

'What *is* it with you? A slow day at the office? You bored with chasing ambulances and courting cripples? Could you not find any butchered Park Avenue debutantes crying over their plastic, misshapen tits?'

'You will not speak to me that way. Desist with this jackassery immediately or you will see a very ugly side of me.'

Miles was out of his chair and standing over me. In hindsight, I should have been concerned about him cracking my skull. I wasn't.

'Did you just say jackassery?'

'I most certainly did.'

We looked at each other for just a moment and I started to smile.

Miles smiled. He put his hands on my shoulder and pulled me up near him. He said, 'Come here.'

We'd only touched once before. He shook my hand when I

graduated from high school. But he felt familiar. I put my head on his chest.

'Your father would be heartbroken if he knew his two favourite people were quarrelling like this.'

'Am I really one of his favourites?'

'You certainly are. When are you going to accept that and stop testing him? When are you going to stop testing everybody? You have many people who care for you despite your best efforts. I didn't mean for this meeting to go this way. But you *do* have a way of bringing out the worst in me sometimes.'

'I'm sorry.'

'I'm sure you are but for the life of me I can't understand why you continue with this mindless behaviour.'

'I do love my father.'

'You hurt him, Rachel. Every time you hurt yourself, you hurt him. I care about you too, you know. Don't forget, I've known you since you were all pigtails and scraped knees. I've gone to great lengths to make sure you're safe and provided for, as your father's attorney; as your father's partner, I've been in an interesting position to help you throughout the years, even if that help has been silent and gone unnoticed. Now here, sit down and talk to me sensibly. Tell me where you're rushing off to now.'

Outside the snow had stopped. The rain had started.

I said, 'I'm going to see Jack.'

'Do you think that is a good idea?'

'I don't know what I think. But I do have this overwhelming feeling that I let the best thing in my life slip away because of pride. Because of some preconceived notion about what a relationship is supposed to be.'

Miles said, 'Consider this, had I been self-involved and persistent, had I subscribed to some fanciful notion of love, then all of our lives would have been much different. If I had insisted that your father leave the family or, on the other hand, if I had indulged him in his fantasies to run away from his responsibilities, what then? Parallel lives such as we've led are not mutually exclusive. In my case, I don't think either would have lasted if the other failed.'

'For the last ten years I've tried to insulate myself from pain. Mainly from the pain of not having Jack in my life when, in actuality, he could have been in my life this whole time. So, I've been self-medicating myself from a phantom affliction that need not exist in the first place.'

'If you think you can salvage things with Jack, build a life with him, then you shouldn't waste another minute in making your way to him. Apologize. Start over and work toward getting yourself under control. But please don't do it labouring under illusions about love. I'm afraid you have grave misconceptions. You think that true love is something that exists without effort, no matter what. But the kind of love you're looking for from both your parents and your lovers only exists at the picture show. True love is exactly the opposite. It requires constant effort and attention. And perhaps most of all it requires compromise and sacrifice. You constantly rail against authority, social norms. And yet your idea of love is so solidly paralysed by popular notions. Love isn't perfect. It isn't a religion.'

'I'm not looking for ecstasy at the foot of an altar or some cataclysmic, earth-shattering experience. All I want is to be enough for one person. For just one person to love me best. I want for one person to like me enough not to want to put his dick into another person.'

'Oh, Rachel. Bless your heart.'

★ ★ ★

When I left New York I had only one thing on my mind: Jack.

Conversation with Gloria.

I called Gloria from the road and asked her to make reservations for a couple of nights at the Wynfrey hotel in Birmingham.

'Starting when?'

'Tonight.'

'You want to go out LaGuardia or JFK?'

'I'm driving not flying.'

'Why in the world would you do that? You'll be exhausted. Are you taking care of your feet?'

'My feet?'

'I knew you wouldn't.'

Conversation with Jack.

'Hello.'

'It's me.'

Jack didn't say anything.

'It's Rachel.'

'Oh, hello you. I can't say it's a surprise. Phillip can't keep a secret.'

'I'm on my way there. Can you meet me tomorrow morning?'

'How long are you in town?'

'Depends.'

'Tomorrow isn't so good. I could meet you Saturday morning before I play golf.'

'It's important.'

'Sure, ok. I'm sorry. It's just that… Well, let me see. You remember the park near Crestline?'

'Yes.'

'I'll be there around ten a.m.'

'Ok.'

Collecting myself.

It was after 3 a.m. when I made it to the Wynfrey.

I watched Dick Van Dyke reruns until the sun came up, ordered waffles from room service and decided to go collect my spoons before I met Jack.

It was an indoor storage facility, air-conditioned, the works. I stood there looking at my things packed neatly. Sitting and waiting for nothing in a climate-controlled environment.

I had to open eleven boxes before I found the spoons. They were in a thin wooden box, cherry-coloured. My grandmother said her first boyfriend gave her that cherry-coloured box. Her first boyfriend wasn't my grandfather. My grandfather was a shortstop for the Cleveland Indians until he went to World War I. When he got back he was a surveyor.

There was a woman vacuuming the hall. I said, 'Excuse me? Hello?'

She pretended not to hear me. I said it louder.

She looked annoyed. But she turned off the vacuum and said, 'What?'

I said, 'Do you know anybody who could use this stuff?'

'What is it?'

'Everything. Nothing.'

'Is there anything I could sell on eBay?'

'Sure. Plenty of that kind of thing.'

That got her attention. She came over to have a look.

She said, 'I've always wanted to sell stuff on eBay.'

'I hear people do quite well for themselves.'

'Have you ever done it?'

'No.'

She said, 'I've got a book on how to.'

'Sounds like you're set then.'

She noticed the box in my hand.

I said, 'This goes with me.'

* * *

Mother's mother was an absolute ball-buster.

Her name was Rita and she served her country as a Navy Nurse in World War I before her country allowed her to vote. She spent her nineteenth birthday stationed in Belgium where she received a Distinguished Service Medal which she sold during the Depression and finished her term on a transport ship.

While in Belgium my grandmother fell in love with a *francs-tireur*. I never knew his name but had reason to believe it was Léon. He gave her the cherry-coloured box. She wouldn't tell me what it originally contained.

But my grandmother left the war and her lover behind, came back to the States, married a surveyor named Wesley Addison and had two children, Vivienne Simone Addison and Felicia Christine Addison.

Mother and her sister weren't close.

My grandparents didn't come around much.

When they did, it was a problem.

Nothing was ever good enough for Mother. She was ashamed for them to see where we lived, although pictures of my grandparents' house showed a modest split-level in Ohio.

Mother was careful to arrange public meetings, usually in the form of an awkward, impersonal dinner out. After my grandfather died, my grandmother came to spend a couple of days with us. This presented a special problem but one that Mother was 100% committed to resolving. She ended up renting a house.

That turned out to be the last time any of us saw my grandmother alive, October, 1979. The visit was a disaster. I kept forgetting where my room was. My grandmother watched from the kitchen as Julie opened every door in the hall trying to find the bathroom. Grandmother cut her visit short by a week. She left three days before my birthday but as a present she gave me her cherry-coloured box full of 50 polished state spoons.

I was impressed. My grandmother had never given any of us a gift before.

The morning after my grandmother left I woke up to a horrible noise in the kitchen. Julie was dropping my spoons into the garbage disposal. She destroyed Mississippi and New Mexico before I tackled her against the refrigerator.

Fruit magnets flew everywhere.

When my grandmother got home, she crushed what was left of my grandfather's morphine prescription and mixed it with applesauce. She gave some to her fifteen-year-old bichon frise (Léon) then she ate the rest. They cuddled up under the duvet and never woke up. She didn't leave a note.

Even as a kid I thought that was a pretty good way to go.

I imagined doing the same.

★ ★ ★

My Aunt Vivienne made it to the funeral home before Mother.

Mother was profoundly disappointed.

It soon became apparent why she was disappointed: she had to take a backseat to the funeral planning.

Mother wasn't good at taking the backseat to anything let alone major things like floral arrangements, casket sprays, song choice and perhaps most importantly, beauty regime for the recently departed. When Mother saw what Vivienne had picked out for my grandmother to wear into eternity, I thought all hell was going to break loose.

Mother said, 'Lavender?'

Vivienne said, 'To the untrained eye, perhaps.'

'What would you call it, dear?'

'It leans subtly to periwinkle in my estimation.'

'Perhaps lavender would have been better, Mother hated periwinkle.'

Vivienne said, 'She did not hate periwinkle.'

'She did. She told me.'

'You're making that up Felicia. Why would you be so cruel at a time like this? Mother's honeymoon dress was periwinkle, you know very well.'

'Yes, I know. That's why she hated it.'

Mother and Vivienne sparred over whether to bury my grandmother wearing her jewellery, wearing her partial dentures, wearing her shoes... all of this while Vivienne's kids fluttered around the house like mad bats.

Mother thought grandmother wouldn't be happy unless buried wearing a girdle.

Vivienne was more in favour of timeless comfort.

They eventually settled on control top pantyhose.

It made me sad.

I liked my grandmother.

Crestline Park.

Jack was waiting for me when I got there.

I knew he would be.

He gave me a hug.

I sat down next to him on a park bench and he said, 'I hear you've been busy lately.'

I laughed.

'Never a dull moment with Rachel. Always drama. At least you can say you're not boring.'

'I guess you've talked to Phillip then.'

'You know he can't keep a secret.'

'It's not really a secret.'

'No? Maybe it should be.'

'You think?'

'It doesn't matter what I think.'

I said, 'Tell me how you're doing?'

'I'm great. Great. Doing just fine. I made partner, you know. Did you know?'

'Yes, Phillip told me. How are *you* doing though?'

He took a drink from a steaming Starbucks to-go cup and apologized. 'I'm sorry. I should have brought you one too. I couldn't remember if you drink coffee. Do you?'

'I do.'

'I'm sorry.'

We were quiet. Children played on the jungle gym. Scattered around the park were clusters of mommies, talking, laughing and some drinking from steaming to-go cups too.

I said, 'How's Joanie?'

'Joanie? She's great. Fine really. She's gone back to school. I think it's more of a break from the kids than anything else. She's studying business. What she's going to do with a handful of business classes, I've no idea. But sure, doing great.'

'How's the whole "married with children" thing treating you?'

'It's all about compromises.'

'You know, after years of spinning my wheels, I have finally come to realize that. Compromises. I've been caught up in the idea of a storybook relationship where love is always enough.'

Jack said, 'Relationships like that don't exist in nature.'

'It's funny though. I suppose I'm hopeless because even then I wanted you to disagree.'

'What was so important that you had to see me this morning?'

'Just this. I was hoping we could talk about our situation.'

'Do we have a situation?'

'Our relationship is what I meant to say. I need to try and explain to you how I felt when all of a sudden, the man I was hoping to marry is with somebody else and asking me to hang around for a good time. That's the way I saw it. All I could hear was an invitation to be your mistress and to me, back then, what that meant was an invitation to be your fool.'

'That was a long time ago.'

'I know but what I'm trying to say is that I shouldn't have been so hasty in dismissing my life with you. We obviously belong together and if that means having to compromise then I'm willing. Leaving you was the worst mistake I ever made.'

'Well, we all make mistakes, don't we? Water under the bridge, all water under the bridge.' He raised his cup and said, 'Here's to the future. Ah, I'm sorry I should have got you one too.'

'No, Jack, listen to me. We could still have a future. I think we could make this work. If anything else I feel more in love with you now than I did. I've done a lot of growing up since then.'

'All that sounds good, really good. We all have to grow up sometime. I'm sure you'll be able to use that positive energy to settle down and rebuild your life. And you know, hey, me and you are always friends.'

A blonde woman wearing a brown suede jacket, a Christmas tree sweater and black tights walked past with a little boy about four years old. She looked at me and said, 'Jack Cohen what are you doing out here in this cold weather?'

Jack was the only one smiling. He said, 'Susan, good to see you. Dennis sell that golf cart yet?'

'Not yet, you interested?'

Jack gave her a business card and said, 'Might be. Have him give me a call.'

She looked at me again and said, 'Tell Joanie I said Merry Christmas.'

'Will do.'

Jack sat back down and said, 'Susan Grossing. Married an engineer who caught her screwing now-husband Dennis up against an entertainment center. Rumour has it that Dennis was wearing her panties.'

'I want to build my life with you.'

Jack didn't say anything. He just stared straight ahead with a semi-smile on his face.

I said, 'Look at me. Don't you love me anymore?'

'Sure. Yes, of course. This isn't the time or place to discuss this. Things are busy for me now. Work is busy. And you've got lots of good things to look forward to, I'm sure. Are you staying in Birmingham or what?'

'I'll stay if you want me to.'

'It's not about what I want. It's what's best for you.'

'You're best for me.'

'I think you should sort yourself out and learn to behave yourself before you make any decisions about what's best for you.'

'I'm telling you as honestly as I can that I still love you and I want to be in your life.'

'I've told you, things are busy. I've got kids now. It's impossible for you to understand how things change when you have kids. There's Joanie. She's trying to make a go at improving herself, or I don't know, gone back to school for a while. Whatever that's all about. And there's work. And there's also, other things too. Other people. But, if you want to stay in Birmingham and get yourself together, settle down and stop all this madness, drugs and other nonsense, well then, I'd be willing to shuffle things and see you sometimes.'

'By "other people" and "other things" do you mean you already have a lover?'

He didn't answer. He finished his coffee and walked over to the garbage can to throw it away.

'Does Joanie know?'

He said, 'Oh, hey… hold on a minute.' He put his hands up to his mouth and shouted, 'Girls! Girls! Ah, hold on a minute. I think they're playing with something dead.'

It never occurred to me that he'd bring his children.

He walked back over with them and said, 'I better get them home and in the tub, these two nasty goats with pigtails.'

Both the girls laughed. Both had bright blue eyes like their daddy. Like their uncle Phillip. Both were missing front teeth. Little girls, out with the only man in their life, the only man who would ever love them unconditionally: Daddy.

And Daddy was here to throw away his old lover, again.

I asked, 'Does Phillip know?'

He gave me his business card and said, 'So, good luck with everything and let me know if you stay in Birmingham.'

He winked and then took the girls to the car.

★ ★ ★

The day the divorce with husband number two was finalized, I went for a drink with my then-attorney.

He said, 'It's rough, catching your sister in bed with your husband.'

I said, 'I was surprised it didn't give me more leverage in the divorce.'

'You'd think, but adultery isn't as weighty in the courts as it used to be. Plus, married such a short time. No kids.'

'I guess.'

He patted my arm. 'I'm going to have another drink, you?'

I said, 'Sure.' He hesitated though. I asked, 'Why are you looking at me like that?'

'Just thinking. I bet you were *really* hot when you were seventeen.'

* * *

The Wynfrey hotel is attached to the Galleria.

The Galleria is a large mall.

They were cleaning my room when I got back to the hotel so I wandered out into the crowd. It was almost Christmas and people were drunk on the fumes of wintergreen potpourri, eyes twitching nervously as they consulted 'to buy' lists.

Christmas lights flashed to near seizure-inducing rhythms, a giant Christmas tree stood under a giant American flag that soared from the ceiling of painted steel girders and massive thermal-insulated plates of glass. Wreaths hung from the girders, along with flying reindeer, stars, ornaments, all reflecting a carousel grinding away while crying children waited in a long line to have their pictures made with Santa.

I waded through the crowd and found a table in the food court. I put my box of spoons in front of me and stared at it.

I thought about Jack.

I thought about my grandmother.

I thought about Julie dropping spoons down the garbage disposal.

Calm descended. I knew what I would do.

I'd collect the two missing spoons in honour of my grandmother and then, I'd kill myself.

The idea of dying made me feel better.

A family was trying to squeeze around the table next to me when the mother asked, 'If you're not using that chair do you mind if my son sits there? It's so busy today. Christmas, eh?'

'Be my guest.'

The little boy must have been about eleven. He was wearing a yellow ski jacket that was so bright it hurt my eyes to look at it. He was sweating.

He ate in silence as long as he could stand it and then he asked, 'What's in the box?'

I said, 'My heart.'

He looked a moment longer and said, 'That box is too small to contain a heart. A human heart is the size of a clenched fist and weighs about twelve ounces. That box is too thin.'

'I was speaking metaphorically.'

He said, 'Oh.'

'You seem to know a lot about the heart. You must be quite intelligent.'

He said, 'I am. I am captain of the scholar bowl team. I had strep throat and couldn't go to the last meet though. So we lost. This girl named Stephanie who thinks she knows everything but really doesn't know anything got SCUBA wrong.'

'What do you mean SCUBA?'

He looked bored by having to explain to yet another plebian. He said, 'SCUBA is an acronym. Do you know what an acronym is? It means that the letters that form the word actually stand for other words. SCUBA stands for self-contained underwater breathing apparatus. AIDS stands for acquired immune deficiency syndrome.'

'Was that one of the other questions?'

'No, you just looked like you needed another example in order to understand.'

I asked, 'Do you have a pen?'

'I always have a pen. But I'll need it back.'

'Certainly.'

I used the pen to write a list on one of his napkins.

List: Things to do before I die.

1. Finish spoon collection. Needed: Mississippi and New Mexico.
2. Figure out how to die.
3. Investigate suicide success rates. Helium a possibility.
4. How difficult to source a helium tank?
5. Call Phillip.

Scorecard: One.

April 22, 1995. I did a stupid thing. Actually, I did two stupid things.

I picked up a hitchhiker.

I got married.

It isn't what it sounds like. I didn't *marry* the hitchhiker, although, unlike the wedding ceremony later in the day, I kept my vow never to do it again.

The hitchhiker: Mary Meringues. I'll never forget that name. She kept spelling it. Mary spoke for 27 minutes without seeming to breathe. I was lulled into a trance.

She was so touched by my act of kindness that she kept showing me her driver's license and promising me that she wasn't a murderer or a kidnapper.

I said, 'I believe you, but I suppose if you are going to kill me it wouldn't matter if I'd seen your license.'

'Why not?'

'I'd be dead.'

Mary said, 'I guess you're right, but still you can't be too careful.' She showed it to me again. M-e-r-i-n-g-u-e-s.

I laughed. She started talking.

'I heard about this one time when a woman was pretending to be pregnant. She wasn't really pregnant though. Her boyfriend was hiding down in the woods so that cars couldn't see him. And what this woman did was raise the hood of her car and sort of wander around the car helpless and crying until somebody stopped. I mean what man in their right mind wouldn't go right ahead and fall for that? A pregnant woman stranded on the side of the road. But these two didn't care about good Samaritans. While she was talking to whoever stopped, the boyfriend would come up out of the woods and knock them in the head with something and then would rob them and sometimes kidnap them and had even killed some of them. All because people thought they were doing something good. Easy as picking apples off the ground. These two said they wasn't sorry either. I mean, what are you going to do with people who can kill somebody just as easy as look at them? Now they're in prison getting three meals a day and watching TV while people like me gotta go out and work for a living.'

I said, 'I suppose that's better than killing for a living.'

Mary said, 'I'm not sure about that sometimes.'

'You realize you aren't building a strong case for yourself. I wonder if your boyfriend is following us at this very moment, waiting for an opportunity to rob me or kill me or worse?'

'What's worse than getting killed?'

'Have you been watching the coverage of the Oklahoma City bombing?'

'No, I can't watch stuff like that. It gives me nightmares.'

My brain turned to oatmeal and was oozing from my ears.

It was my own fault. People shouldn't be encouraged. My motto should be: Don't feed the animals!

It reminded me of the time my father took us all to Safari on Wheels. It was a sickly park that boasted exotic outdoor adventures from the comfort and safety of your own car. It had a great expanse of open land with animals roaming free. They made you sign a waiver and a declaration that under no circumstances would you exit your car or feed the animals. Everywhere you looked there were huge Safari on Wheels signs reminding visitors of this pact.

Julie was throwing stale bagels out the window and Mother was screaming at her, 'Don't feed the animals.'

Eventually a crowd of squalling gibbons jumped on the car. Mother went into hysterics when two of them started making gibbon babies on the bonnet.

★ ★ ★

Three days after the Oklahoma City Bombing I married Andy Maupin.

He reminded me of tofu.

He absorbed the flavour of whatever was round him.

Not surprisingly, people liked him.

Andy was an oral and maxillofacial surgeon. He didn't like it. He would have been happy with a small town, general practice: handing out toothbrushes after routine cleans and referring root canals.

That wasn't good enough for his family.

I didn't marry just Andy. I married the whole clan.

They were a group of egotistic infants masquerading as sophisticated adults. They moved in the same social circle as Mother which meant they were mostly concerned with my stock portfolio. I wasn't sure if I was engaged or up for auction. I imagined Mother handing out business cards and droning on and on... *Rachel comes with acreage and twenty goats.*

Andy's grandfather, Lucas Maupin, was the only one who didn't give a damn about my *dowry.* He was more interested in whether I'd make good breeding stock. He was forever sizing up the suitability of my child-bearing hips and trying to assess the state of my teeth and gums.

★ ★ ★

Lucas grew up poor, working ranches in Bosque County, Texas.

If he told me once, he told me a hundred times, 'That's Bosque. Pronounced Bahs-key.'

Lucas took things upon himself.

Andy let him.

It wasn't unusual to wake up to the sound of Lucas mowing our grass or hammering a loose shingle. I came home one afternoon to find him up a tree. He was wearing a pair of caulks and a pink hard hat. He had one arm roped around a branch and the other arm extended to full length, swinging a chainsaw at one of the limbs. Woodchips snowed down. As I stood watching a limb fell on the shed out back.

Lucas shouted down, 'Needed rebuilding anyway.'

I went into the kitchen and a few minutes later Lucas stuck his head around the corner and asked, 'Is Andy all right?'

'I haven't talked to him today but I'm sure he is.'

'No, I mean all right all right.'

'Yes sir. He's fine.'

'I mean, is he all right in the sack?'

'Why do you ask?'

'Hell, I was afraid of that.'

'That wasn't an answer. I was just curious why you were asking such a personal question.'

'Be honest with me. Is he shooting blanks? You can get doctors to check that stuff you know.'

'I'm sure his "stuff" is fine.'

'If he was fine you'd have me some grandchildren by now.'

I didn't tell Lucas that I was the problem, not Andy. He seemed to have such confidence in my shiny coat and pretty tail feathers that I didn't have the heart to break his faith in such things.

★ ★ ★

The first time Andy and I had sex he said, 'Open your mouth again.'

I did.

He asked, 'Have you had your wisdom teeth out?'

'No.'

'You've definitely got some overcrowding issues.'

★ ★ ★

We decided to call it quits sometime just before I had emergency surgery for an ovarian torsion and just after our third wedding anniversary.

When I woke up from surgery Andy wasn't there but my father was and so were Lucas and Anne.

I said, 'You didn't have to drive all this way to see me.'

Anne said, 'Oh, we didn't. One of our deacons had a pacemaker put in and we came to see him and we thought, well… we're here. Might as well.'

I was still groggy from the anaesthesia but the last thing I heard was Anne telling my father, 'We didn't think it would last this long. God's will be done.'

Lucas said, 'Amen.'

Sorrow, thou knowest me.

On the way out of Birmingham I stopped for gas.

A man asked if I could spare some change.

I said, 'I'm sorry. I don't have any cash.'

He looked at the BMW.

I said, 'I'm paying for the gas with a card. Unless you don't mind change? Do you mind change?'

'I don't mind anything, lady.'

I opened the trunk and unzipped my travel bag. All my things from rehab were still packed. I took out my money pouch and opened it wide, showing him all the Connecticut quarters.

I said, 'I don't know why I keep them. I tell people that they keep me safe but I don't believe that.'

He didn't care why I had them.

I said, 'Hold out your hands.'

He let three of them drop without picking them up. He walked away.

'Aren't you going to say thank you?'

He said, 'Lady, you're outta luck if you're looking to me to feel good about yourself. Fuck, you're driving a hundred-thousand-dollar car and you fucking give me a handful of change. Don't expect me to be your dancing pony. Ho fucking ho.'

★ ★ ★

As I left the gas station I thought: one hell of a coincidence or there's a guy in a Lincoln Navigator following me.

★ ★ ★

My cell phone rang. It was my father.

He asked, 'Where are you?'

I looked in the rearview mirror and said, 'I suspect you already know.'

'How did the meeting with Jack go?'

'I'm sure you know that too.'

'Do you have plenty of money?'

'Yes.'

He said, 'Do you have any interest in opening an art gallery in Los Angeles?'

'I don't know anything about art.'

'You could learn.'

'Why do you ask?'

'I met with a Mister Itokawa this week and his son is an artist. He's looking for a platform to launch his work in the States. And I thought that when you're done with this little escapade we could discuss your future.'

'When I'm done with this "little escapade" there'll be no need to discuss my future.'

'What does that mean?'

'Nothing.'

I took the exit for I20/I59. So did the Navigator.

★ ★ ★

For a while people thought Julie and I were deaf and dumb.

It was an easy mistake.

As we settled into the country club mentality, rumours began amongst the upper crust that the Bennett girls were 'off'.

I blame the problem and the cure on a surge in popularity of made-for-television Victorian era movies. I despised the Brontës.

Mother said, 'Little girls should be seen not heard.'

I said, 'What about big girls?'

'Big girls are an entirely different matter and questions like that are exactly the reason why you should say nothing if you can't say something nice.'

'How was that not nice?'

'When we have company, keep your mouths shut, the both of you. Adults don't like to be grilled by children nor do they enjoy hearing your foolish stories and certainly don't tell them anything about me.'

Julie said, 'Whatever will *you* talk about then?'

Mother said, 'Don't be like your sister.'

So we kept quiet. We didn't speak even when spoken to. That is until Tippy Embry asked Mother (as delicately as she could and within earshot of both Julie and me) about the condition of her poor girls.

Mother said, 'What condition?'

'Are they slow?'

Barnum Bailey couldn't have erected the big top faster than Mother sprang into action. It was circus lights, flying trapeze, no nets!

She had us performing every time we had company. We became a novelty of another sort then. It wasn't that the first rumour was dispelled. It was more like we were considered reformed. More: look dear, the deaf and dumb girls have been taught to sing and play piano.

Julie frequently performed Shakespeare, in particular *Julius Caesar*.

My excerpts from Alexander Pope's *The Dunciad* were somewhat less popular.

★ ★ ★

Jim Yancy liked living in our pool house.

His official capacity: Artist in Residence.

Mother commissioned him to paint our portraits. He started with Julie and me.

We'd sit for hours and hours while he marauded around the room. Slapping paint onto the canvas and then grumbling about the lighting.

I said, 'Why have we got to pose together?'

Julie said, 'Because Mother has one empty place above the fireplace not two.'

'What about that big wall by the piano?'

'That's where her portrait is going.'

Jim was in lust with Julie. She was sixteen and pretty and venomous: his type. He was forever suggesting amendments to her posture as we posed. 'Beautiful, could you reach down there and slightly adjust your left breast. Yeah, just give it a jiggle up toward the other one.'

Julie fell for it a couple of times.

Mother borrowed a Shi Tzu from her bridge partner for her portrait. The dog's name was Manny. Manny hated Mother with a passion. It was rare that a session passed without the Shi Tzu drawing blood.

The resulting portrait was grossly abstract. Mother wasn't pleased. She refused to pay Jim for it but I heard some time later that it was auctioned as part of a larger group of his work, fetching $36,000 alone.

It wasn't long after he completed Mother's portrait that Jim completely lost his mind. If not his mind, then certainly his cool. He began experimenting with his art and drugs. The pool house looked like a blood bath. Red paint splashed all over the walls.

He even tried painting with his penis. I was impressed but Julie and Mother were horrified. My father didn't know until he heard Jim ask me if I knew what a fluffer was.

My father had Jim's things packed and ready to go when Jim returned from yoga.

When I went to the pool house Jim was staring at the labelled cardboard boxes and pouring Worcestershire sauce on sliced loaf bread.

He said, 'You want one?'

I said, 'Nah, I'm not hungry.'

'About last night, all that fluffer talk, I wasn't really going do anything to you.'

'I don't think you knew what you were doing.'

'Maybe you're right.'

'Do you suppose you'll die from doing drugs?'

'I doubt it. My old man lived to be ninety-seven. I have high hopes of being a drain on the healthcare system for a long time.'

Jim lit a joint and sat down.

I asked him where he was planning to go.

'I don't know.'

I said, 'Why don't you get a place of your own?'

'I don't like to be alone.'

'Perhaps you'll meet somebody nice and get married.'

'I'd rather get the plague. Hand me that roach clip.'

★ ★ ★

Jim made it as far as the real redhead's Spanish *hacienda* next door. She wanted to support the arts too.

★ ★ ★

Eight years old: my father took me fishing.

We bought the following things:

1. Two rod and reels
2. Hooks
3. Sinkers
4. Two fold-out chairs
5. Two cheeseburgers (ketchup only) and two large fries
6. One Styrofoam cup of red worms

When we got to the water, we ate lunch. Set up our chairs. My father skewered a red worm on my hook. He baited his hook.

He showed me how to cast. I cast for the first time and sunk the snelled fishing hook into my father's forearm.

I watched while he tried to get it out. I asked, 'Can I call you Louis?'

He said, 'No.'

'That's your name isn't it?'

'Not as far as you're concerned.'

'Dad?'

'What Rachel?'

'I'm really sorry about hooking you.'

'I know but you still can't call me Louis.'

'That's ok. I didn't really want to.'

★ ★ ★

I tried to imagine death. My worst fear was failing or being saved.

If I succeeded, I didn't want to leave a mess for somebody else to clean up.

There were a lot of factors to consider.

Made a note to self: wonder if suffocation by duct-taping whole head would work?

Scorecard: Two.

October 8, 1999: Kevin Alexander.

I met Kevin while he was roofing my apartment building. He was very handsome, very fit and if one was inclined to do such a thing, one could have bounced a quarter off his ass.

Kevin owned his own beer keg and he had a collection of ice bongs. As a wedding present, his friends chipped in and bought me a torch pipe shaped in the likeness of a large, mahogany-coloured penis.

Our wedding was exceptional in that it turned into a tribute to Gorilla Monsoon who died two days before. Immediately after we were introduced to the 'congregation' as man and wife, two of Kevin's friends reenacted the 1977 Puerto Rican match between (legendary) Gorilla Monsoon and André the Giant.

André won.

Kevin didn't let being married affect his dating scene. I gained weight. The more weight I gained the more he fooled around. The more he fooled around, the more weight I gained.

We were married five months. The divorce followed soon after I found him having sex with my sister.

Julie said, 'I didn't think you would mind.'

I said, 'You could have asked first.'

Therapy: A Monologue.

Characters:
Dr Gabriel Holden (Dr): New Psychiatrist
Rachel (R): Old Patient

Dr: Come in, Rachel. I'm Gabriel. It's nice to meet you. Let's see, where shall we sit? Are you more comfortable by the desk or the window?

R: Doesn't matter.

Dr: Let's go for the widow seat.

R: Are you a big Thomas the Tank Engine fan?

Dr: Excuse me?

R: This was in the chair.

Dr: Oh, here. I'm sorry. Let me take that. My daughter was in earlier today. If I've stepped on one of these little metal trains I've stepped on a hundred. You should see the top of our coffee table. It's a full-blown rail yard.

R: I would have been beheaded if I went near Mother's furniture with a toy.

Dr: I suppose we should be a bit more stringent about things like that but we try to be realists. Accidents are bound to happen. Most of our furniture came from the second-hand shops. Maybe if we have any money left when the little rascal gets out of college we'll redecorate the house. Do you have children?

R: No.

Dr: I don't blame you. I haven't slept in six years. I've read your file. I know you've seen Doctor Vickarman for quite a while and I can imagine such an abrupt transition might pose a problem for you but Doctor Vickarman had issues of a personal nature that required her to take immediate leave from the practice. And so, here we are.

R: I don't mind not seeing Doctor Vickarman any more. I'm not sure what I was getting out of it anyway. It was pretty much: show up, spar and get a handful of new prescriptions. I'm not even sure that I want to continue therapy. I'm even less sure about all this medication I'm taking.

Dr: Let's take it slowly, ok? I am not really of the 'let's hit the ground running' mindset when it comes to new patients. And by that I simply mean there's a lot I need to try to understand about where you're coming from before we start making radical changes in things like medication. Is that ok with you?

R: Yes.

Dr: How about for today you just tell me a little about yourself.

R: What do you want to know?

Dr: Anything.

R: Um… I'm a plain oatmeal kind of girl. Just butter and sugar. I don't go out of the house much any more. I feel happier when people can't see me. For the most part people make me want to shove bamboo up my nose. Is this the kind of thing you want to know?

Dr: It's great. Keep going.

R: I can't sing although I do. I can't dance although I do that too. I've been told that a toadstool has more rhythm. I've been married and divorced four times. I have the emotional IQ of a fencepost because I'm only a year out of yet another destructive, pointless relationship that's left me out of work and broke and eating tranquillizers and antidepressants like they're Chiclets. I tend to thoughtlessly get myself involved with men who aren't right for me and then thoughtfully stay in the relationship until we're both proverbially battered and bruised beyond recognition. When these relationships are over I spend a great deal of energy feeling stupid and wondering why I can't break the habit of breaking the habit. At this point I'm no longer functioning like a typical human being or, I don't know, perhaps I'm functioning too much like a typical human being. Stupidity and cruelty in others and in myself make me want to die. And I don't mean that in a metaphorical way. I spend a large portion of my days lost in suicide fantasies which sadly enough seem to be the only thing which comforts me. I feel a profound guilt over ending the relationship with the only man I've ever passionately loved. Although at the time, in my haste and immaturity, I felt certain that he'd left me no choice. And perhaps he didn't. Either way, in subsequent years I've no doubt idealized and romanticized the relationship well and truly out of proportion. I hate myself for being weak. I feel intense anger at my mother for being harsh and selfish and for sacrificing what might have been best for me for what would comfort her. I feel intense anger at my father for being sweet and absent and for sacrificing what might have been best for me for what made him happy. I feel intense guilt on both counts because I know that parents are only human. I know they love me. I feel powerless and self-conscious and ill-equipped to deal with and interpret my own emotions. And so for all these things I feel the need to be both saved and punished. I have, in the not so distant past, tried to ease these extreme emotions with equally extreme remedies: bingeing, cutting, drugs, matrimony. I don't like pain but then again when I am that strung out I don't really feel pain in a traditional way. I'm pretty sure in some cases at least that I harm myself to keep from taking a tire iron to other people. I'm a walking, talking contradiction. Nothing I say stays true for very long and perhaps that is intentional. A girl once told me that people want to be understood but they don't want to be figured out. I think that, even though she wore a sheet over her head and had a taste for drinking gasoline, she was probably right. Nothing truly bad has ever happened to me. I feel weak for not being able to handle my life. I'm sorry. I have no idea where all of that came from. Well, yes I do. But I'm still sorry. I'm sure we're out of time.

Dr: Don't worry about it. They can wait.

M-I-crookedlettercrookedletter-I-crookedlettercrookedletter-I-humpbackhumpback-I.

That's how Ms Milton, my first grade teacher, taught me to spell Mississippi.

Mother said, 'That's good. Can you spell it right, too?'

Julie said, 'All people who ride the short bus spell it that way.'

I said, 'I don't ride the short bus.' At the time I didn't know what it meant to ride the short bus but I do now.

★ ★ ★

First stop: Mississippi.

I didn't have a plan. I knew I needed a Mississippi spoon. Mississippi is one state west of Alabama. I started driving.

I stopped at a Stuckey's in Meridian. It wasn't the Stuckey's I remembered from childhood. This one was multi-tasking: ATM, Chevron and Subway sandwich shop as well. I bought a tank of gas, a variety box of salt water taffy, a pecan log and a State of Mississippi collector's spoon all under the same roof.

I've never spent any appreciable time in Mississippi. I do admit to visiting one of the American Indian Reservation casinos. It was as far removed from the Las Vegas experience as possible. I went with Daniel and he would have driven right past the place if I hadn't noticed the Pay and Play All Day Buffet sign. Within half an hour, we lost all our money, ate lukewarm Salisbury Steak and were back on the road home.

At the meeting of I20 and I55, I stopped at Jackson to see Eudora Welty's house. I'd never been much of a tourist before but I thought: what the hell.

I wasn't terribly surprised by anything I saw there. I didn't really see much though. It wasn't open to general public viewings and I wasn't allowed to join the group tour just starting because it was limited to twelve people. I would have made it thirteen.

The man conducting the tour told me that if I would be patient I could join them for the garden tour. He said, 'Are you able to negotiate uneven terrain?'

I said, 'Yes sir. I've made a career out of it.'

'You can give me the two dollars fifty in cash.'

'Why would I give you two dollars fifty?'

'The cost of the whole tour is five dollars.'

'And you want me to give you two dollars fifty to see the garden we're standing in?'

'There's more to it than this.'

'How much more?'

He said, 'The trouble with people like you is that you're always trying to get something for nothing.'

'Interesting but I've had more experience with nothing for something. I'll pass on the tour.'

'Suit yourself.' He pointed to a sign.

The sign said: No Photography. No Loitering.

I looked at an old couple sitting on a bench and said, 'What about them?'

He had already walked away by that time but he did give me a single-fingered gesture in parting.

The old couple was fighting. At least, one out of the two was fighting.

The woman was mad.

The man was reading a brochure.

She said, 'Karl, why are you so quiet? Are you still sulking about last night? Is that it? I warned you about this, for sixty-two years I've warned you about this. And you know what? This just proves my point. It proves my point, Karl. The key to a happy marriage is never go to bed angry! And what did you do last night?'

Karl wasn't answering but I give him credit for knowing that he was standing on a rhetorical land mine.

'I'll tell you what you did! You went to bed angry, that's what you did. After sixty-two years, you went to bed angry. Do you not listen to a single word I say?'

Karl was still reading the brochure.

'Karl!'

'What?'

'You don't listen to a single word I say!'

'I hear most of them. Do I have to listen too?'

I couldn't help it. I laughed.

You would have thought that her neck was spring-loaded the way she snapped a look at me.

She said, 'Why you impudent little so-and-so. You better mind your manners before somebody slaps you into next week.'

I said, 'That might be true but it sure won't be you.'

'Believe you me you don't want to pick a fight with me. Does she Karl?'

I said, 'I'm sure you're a real firecracker, ma'am, but victory is merely an illusion when it comes to war and using the last square of toilet paper. Somebody's arse is gonna get chapped one way or t'other.'

Karl laughed.

★ ★ ★

For a while Mother thought about giving Julie a coming-out party.

After our experience at the Botanical Gardens she decided Julie was 'out' enough.

At the time, Julie was seventeen and I was fourteen. Mother was invited to attend a baby shower at the Gardens and she wanted to use the opportunity for us to be 'seen'. We all three spent a day at the spa: manicures, pedicures, cut, colour, fried, dried, laid to the side, and make-up. The works. Julie even got plucked.

Mother wore lavender linen. Julie wore white linen. I wore chartreuse linen.

Apparently linen was the thing to wear to baby showers at the Botanical Gardens.

Chartreuse wasn't my colour. Chartreuse isn't anybody's colour. The dress also had three-quarter sleeves. It took years of therapy to acknowledge the horror and get on with my life.

We hadn't been there ten minutes when Mother had an accident with a shrimp and avocado canapé. While she was in the bathroom, Julie took the opportunity to tell anybody who would listen (and there were plenty) that I was pregnant too and that the father was the Cookies pest control man who came to spray our house for termites.

I had no idea about this until, later that night, my father came up to my room with a cup of hot chocolate for me and what looked like a double scotch for him. He said, 'Darling, is there anything we need to talk about?'

'Yes, the news is saying there's at least nine dead from this tornado in Barneveld, Wisconsin.'

I turned the volume up on the television and we watched until my father said, 'No, darling. Is there anything else we need to talk about?'

'Like what?'

'What about the pest control man?'

'What about him?'

★ ★ ★

When I got back to my car the guy driving the Navigator was reading a copy of the Jackson Advocate.

I tapped on the window.

He rolled it down.

I said, 'This is a nice vehicle.'

He said, 'Thanks.'

'Is it a company car?'

'Sort of.'

'How much is my father paying you to follow me?'

'Quite a lot.'

'What is your name?'

'Noah.'

'Write your cell phone number down for me.'

'Ok.'

'You ready to roll?'

'I'm ready when you are.'

'Let's hit it.'

★ ★ ★

Information:

The National Lightning Safety Institute: (on average) 1,000 lightning strike victims per year in the United States.

The Central Intelligence Agency's World Fact Book: population in the United States approximately 303,824,640.

Round off.

1/304,000 chance of getting struck by lightning.

Further.

You're more likely to get struck by lightning than you are likely to purchase a fresh Bear Claw pastry at a gas station.

★ ★ ★

Once we were back on the road, I called Noah.

I said, 'Start at the beginning.'

'Start at the beginning?'

'Tell me everything about yourself.'

'I don't know where to begin.'

'Does the beginning not work for you?'

'It's difficult to know what to include and what to leave out.'

I suggested that we play the Question Game. Not being

familiar with the Question Game (a.k.a. interrogation) he agreed. I promised to help him if need be.

I asked, 'When were you born?'

Noah said, 'October 26, 1972. I'm a Water Rat.'

'I'm a Flying Mongoose.'

'No, that's my Chinese sign. When were you born?'

'October 31, 1969.'

'You're an Earth Rooster.'

'Do you have that stuff memorized?'

'Yes.'

'Do those two signs get along?'

'Probably not very well.'

'I would have guessed not. Another: what colour is your toothbrush?'

'Blue.'

'Scooby Doo: Pre or post Scrappy?'

'Definitely pre Scrappy.'

'Have you ever been in prison?'

'No. Have you?'

'I'm supposed to be asking the questions.'

Noah said, 'Yes then.'

I asked, 'Ginger or Mary Ann?'

'Both, different days.'

'Figures. Right or left?'

'Right.'

'Do you have any brothers and sisters?'

'Yes. Five brothers. Three sisters.'

'Holy hell. Nine kids altogether?'

'My parents couldn't afford central heating. They had to stay warm somehow.'

And that's how my conversation with Noah began. He was born in Washington State, the second of nine children. Those nine children eventually produced eleven grandchildren. His mother and two oldest sisters were all pregnant at the same time.

Noah: not married/no children.

I said, 'How you could *stand* growing up with that many people in the house?'

'Ah, it wasn't that bad. Modesty was a survival tool. Growing up with that many brothers and sisters made it impossible to be too precious. If you couldn't handle brutal honesty, it was game over.'

'Brutal honesty, huh? That wouldn't have won the popular vote at my house. I didn't know what truth was until I made it up.'

Noah laughed. He said, 'My mom had all her children at home. My Aunt Grace is a licensed midwife.'

'Great. Must have been the equivalent of having a car salesman for a brother.'

'I watched my first live birth when I was six. Believe me, after that it's difficult to harbour any antiseptic illusions about life. I think it's really shaped my view of the world, being with my mom and experiencing her pain and joy. '

'I can imagine. No, actually I can't. I'm pretty sure Mother would abort me *now* if she had a chance.'

We were quiet for a moment. Noah said, 'Did I lose you?'

'No. I'm still here. You seem like a nice guy, Noah. Why are you out here chasing your boss's daughter?'

'Because he asked me to.'

'Do you do everything he asks you to?'

'This seemed particularly important to him.'

'Why did he pick you?'

'Maybe he thought we'd get along.'

'I doubt it. Did you go to college?'

'Washington State.'

'What was your major?'

'Human Development.'

'That explains a lot. Let's stop in Shreveport for the night. I'm hanging up now.'

We spent the night at a place called The 20 Winx Lodge.

It was a far cry from The Four Seasons but the teenaged girl who checked us in was proud to point out that Triple A had given them a two-star rating.

The office was finished with walnut-coloured wood panelling and everything else was done in a 1970s colour palette – avocado green, burnt umber, and harvest gold. It was clear that this was a family owned and operated establishment. Several things pointed to this conclusion but especially the cross-stitched sign above the entrance to their living quarters which read: Family owned and operated establishment.

While the girl checked us in the sound of a loud television and two little boys made it almost impossible to hear her. And every few minutes the mother would shout at them to quiet down while Lisa got the guests checked in. She kept telling them not to be so loud, that it was rude.

'Lisa, you want ketchup and mustard?'

The girl screamed back, 'Just ketchup.'

The father came in carrying a box of brochures for the lodge. He introduced himself and gave us one.

The girl said, 'They're already checking in. Why are you giving them one?'

The father seemed embarrassed by her lack of marketing savvy and said, 'They might have some friends that might like to come stay.'

The mother's voice from the back said, 'Gill, is that you? Dinner's ready.'

'You folks enjoy your stay.'

He went into the back room and the television was turned off and everything was quiet except the sound of plates and forks. Then the mother screamed, 'Lisa! Did you drive the car today?'

The father said, 'Hush up, she's got people in there.'

'I don't care if the President of the United States of America is in there.' The mother came around the corner wiping her hands on a cloth. 'S'cuse me folks. Answer me, Lisa. Did you drive that car today after me telling you not to?'

'No.'

'No? No? You got the nerve to stand there and lie to me about it? You want to know how your daddy knows it was you? Cigarette ashes everywhere! Now, you can sneak off and give yourself cancer if you want to! You can smell like an ashtray and ruin your fingernails and ruin your complexion if you want to! But you're not going to ruin the Plymouth!'

Lisa continued to process the credit card. She wrote out a receipt.

The mother said, 'I'm sorry folks. You got kids? You'll understand, if you do.' She examined the receipt Lisa was working on and asked, 'Why you charging them so much for?'

'Cos they're getting two rooms.'

The mother looked back at us and gave us a knowing smile. She said, 'Listen, it's Christmas and all. You ought to save your money if it's really just one room you gone use. We are discreet around here.'

I said, 'Oh, no ma'am. We're not together.'

Noah said, 'She snores like a lumberjack!'

'I do not!'

The woman smiled and went back to her supper.

Lisa said, 'Sorry about all this. You're in nineteen and twenty. Nineteen's got a little Christmas tree.'

I asked if there were any good places to eat around there and Lisa said, 'Sure. Go out to the main road, go left and you'll get to Dairy Queen, Taco Bell, Denny's and ah, Waffle House. If you go right back toward the interstate, you'll get to the new KFC that's in with the gas station.'

Once outside I asked, 'How did you know that I snore like a lumberjack?'

'I didn't until now.'

★ ★ ★

I tried to imagine what it would be like for a family of eleven to live under a single roof.

When I was seventeen Jack and I got into a bit of trouble and had to do community service.

I was sentenced to 72 hours at a nonprofit organization for single mothers. It was very 'a journey of a thousand miles begins with one step' type stuff. Some of my time there was spent in the nursery. They established a programme called Mommy's Day Out, where single moms got a break from their kids to do whatever they want to.

One day they talked me into dressing up like Minnie Mouse. I scared the children to death. One little girl went into hysterics.

They moved me after that.

★ ★ ★

No surprise, I couldn't sleep.

I stayed as long as I could stand it. Then had to go. It would be better anyway. I couldn't really finish my plan with my happy little shadow, Noah, following me.

I decided to leave him.

I sat in the car looking at his dark window. The lodge reminded me of Christmas, 1977. We hadn't seen my father in a couple of weeks because he had been away on business so Mother had planned a big Christmas. She'd rented a cabin in Tennessee and my father was supposed to meet us there.

We went up the day before Christmas to get the place ready. The people she rented the place from had left the key in the mailbox, just like they said they would but beyond that, their description of the place was very generous. Mother's grand expectations were floundering.

The custom kitchen turned out to be little more than a deluxe hotplate. The Jacuzzi had a note taped to the side expressing concern over an incident of 'mild' electrocution. There was no running water and no indoor plumbing which was a problem for us but didn't seem to bother the raccoon nesting in what was supposed to be my room.

I have to say, I was quite proud of the way Mother took these things in her stride. She decided that she wasn't going to let circumstances disturb our happy Christmas. We drove into Chattanooga to a fancy hotel to see the Christmas lights and to get our pictures made with Santa Claus. Even though Mother was putting on a brave face, I did notice that she tried to bribe the front desk clerk into booking a room. Eventually the manager came around and insisted that we leave.

Mother wanted to get a Christmas tree but the lot where the Kiwanis Club had been selling them was empty except for the occasional shorn branch and trimmed trunk. Undaunted, Mother handed Julie over into the dumpster at the back of the lot where she retrieved one of their cast-off trees.

The main grocery store was closed but Mother managed to find a small store still open and we decorated the tree with things from there including but not limited to goldfish crackers, popcorn, Captain Crunch cereal and dates stuffed with cream cheese which reminded me of roaches.

Mother managed to build a fire, although it wasn't really cold enough for a fire. I slept on the couch so as not to disturb the raccoon, although, at some point during the night the raccoon came out of my room and feasted upon the Christmas tree ornaments. I half-heartedly tried to stop it but it hissed at me with such vehemence that I quickly adopted a 'well, it's Christmas' attitude and let the little woodland creature eat in peace.

My father never showed up and because he was supposed to bring Mother's gifts, she didn't have anything from us to open on Christmas morning. She assumed the role of martyr and we opened our gifts in silence. When I opened a handheld Space

Invaders game and asked if we had any batteries, Julie pinched me and shook her head.

Mother cried.

That night we all slept in Mother's bed while the raccoon finished off what was left on the Christmas tree.

My father was at home when we got back and said he thought the cabin was booked over New Years' not Christmas. Mother was inconsolable. Not even the little blue box from Tiffany's was enough to make her feel better.

She told him to take it back. She was sure Gloria still had the receipt.

★ ★ ★

It's amazing how things work but once I left the hotel in Shreveport and started driving, I became almost instantly drowsy.

I only made it for about three hours before I had to pull over at a rest stop somewhere near Mesquite, Texas.

I pulled the car under an orange security light and sat there for a moment trying to decide what to do. Sure, the chances of me getting kidnapped, robbed, raped or murdered or some combination of any or all of those things was high. But falling asleep while barrelling down the interstate at ninety miles per hour had disadvantages as well. The disadvantages mainly concerned whatever poor fool I would run head-long into, so, after weighing my options, I decided to stay put. I couldn't care less what happened to me.

I closed my eyes and fell sound asleep.

I didn't bother to lock the doors.

★ ★ ★

I woke up a couple of hours later, it was already light outside.

I got out and stretched my legs.

I walked to the bathroom and found a truck driver there, writing on the walls. When he saw me he said, 'Sorry, the gents' is broken.'

'By broken, do you mean all the prime wall space is already covered with graffiti?'

He realized he was still holding a black marker mid-air and he smiled. 'Just spreading the word.'

He held up his finger as if to tell me to wait one second. He wrote a few lines and then said, 'Sorry to disturb you.'

I laughed and said, 'Don't worry about it. I was disturbed long before I came in here.'

The truck driver left and I couldn't help but look to see what was so important for him to come into the women's toilet to write on the wall. What I saw, I interpreted to be a fairly crude rendition of childbirth. A close-up drawing of legs akimbo. Below that was written, For God so loved the world he gave... John 3.16.

I walked to one of the stalls and noticed a sign upon which was written *Please don't eat the urinal cakes. The Management.*

When I came out there was a woman washing her hands and I pointed to the sign and said, 'Why do you suppose they use the word "cake" if they didn't want to tempt people into having a taste?'

She said, 'I don't know but you probably shouldn't try it.'

'I wasn't going to eat it. I just thought the sign was ironic.' She stared at me until I said, 'Never mind.'

She said, 'I don't have any money.'

'Ok.'

'I'm serious, not a penny. God as my witness.'

I finished washing my hands and said, 'I'm not going to give you money, if that's what you're after.'

'Are you not going to rob me?'

'Rob you?'

'Yeah.'

'I wasn't planning on robbing you. Will you be terribly

disappointed if I don't?'

'I'm not *that* way either.'

'And what way is that?'

'Lesbianed.'

I looked at her. I imagined beating her in the mouth with a bat, red splatter patterns flecking the walls in a macabre fresco.

She looked at me, deadpan. I felt slack and expressionless, just like her. It made me tired.

I suddenly felt hungry for something chocolate.

★ ★ ★

When I came back to my car, Noah was there.

I asked him how he found me.

'I don't really have to "find" you. The satellite navigation has a tracking device.'

'This is all a bit too much for me, Noah. So, right now. Right this minute. What do I do? Do I beat the hell out of you and run?'

'I suppose you could try.'

'Please, stop following me.'

'I can't. But I could stay at a distance. We don't have to talk or interact in any way.'

'But you'd *still* be following me!'

Is there a Third Option?

Mother once told me: Do as I say, not as I do.

I said, 'Is there a third option?'

My lifespan has been cut short by the stupidity of others.

At some point and time in my life, I've heard people use the following statements.

If it was up to me, they would be pistol-whipped.

1. You're just blowing smoke up my ass.
2. Who pissed in your cornflakes this morning?
3. It's colder than a witch's tit, wearing a brass bra and doing push-ups in the snow.
4. Does a bear shit in the woods?
5. Who pulled your chain?
6. Don't start nothing, won't be nothing.
7. I'm about to open up a can of whoop ass.
8. He might not suck a dick but he'd hold it in his mouth until the swelling went down.
9. Slicker than snot on a door knob.
10. I've got to take a dump.
11. I've got to drain my lizard.
12. She's tighter than a gnat's ass.
13. Shit or get off the pot.
14. They're all pink on the inside.
15. Happy as a pig in shit.
16. Full as a tick.
17. Hotter than two rats fucking in a wool sock.
18. His voice makes my ass want to suck a lemon.
19. Don't get your panties in a wad.
20. Don't pee on my leg and tell me it's raining.

* * *

The only physical fight I've ever been in started over a cliché.

I was eight years old and it was a beautiful summer afternoon.

We were playing outside when all of a sudden Mother came running out the front door. She was screaming. Her attention seemed to be fixated on the roof.

Turned out, she had been trying to take a nap and a red-headed woodpecker was feverishly pecking away at one of the vinyl-clad gutters.

We didn't know that at the time.

I can't say it would have mattered if we did.

Mother came outside, looking up at the top of the house, waving her arms and screaming, 'Shoo! Shoo! You annoying bastard! Get away! Get away!'

She repeated that several times.

She even tried shaking one of the lower branches of a Dogwood tree.

Jack said, 'What's she doing?'

I said, 'Don't know.'

Darla Jones, a freckled husk of a nightmarish little girl said, 'She's crazy.'

I said, 'She is not.'

'Yeah, she is. My mother says so. My mother says that the acorn doesn't fall far from the tree.'

I wasn't terribly concerned what Darla Jones or her mother thought about *my* mother. On a good day I would have happily joined in a calm discussion about the state of Mother's mental health. But the fact that anybody would ever compare me to her, let alone insinuate that we might be alike, well, no court in the land would hold me accountable for my actions.

I picked up a Wiffle ball bat and started beating Darla Jones about the head and neck.

Jack finally managed to get the bat away from me and Darla Jones ran home to tell her mother that she'd been attacked.

Jack said, 'You're gonna be in trouble.'

I said, 'I don't care.'

'Have you been practising your swing?'

'No.'

'It's good.'

'Thanks.'

Scorecard: Three.

February 29, 2000: Lance Harmon.
Leap year.

Something seemed terribly appropriate about marrying Lance on a day that only exists once every four years.

He was a forensic pathologist specializing in entomology. Lance was passionate about three things: larvae growth in cadavers, Dungeons and Dragons, and performing at Renaissance festivals with a travelling band of minstrels called the Willing Rogues. Lance played the psaltery.

The whole time we were together we only had two real fights. One started over a misunderstanding about the differences between empusids and hymenopodids. The other began after he revealed that he had a heightened sense of smell.

I said, 'Have you ever thought of being a superhero?'

He said, 'That's not funny Rachel. It isn't easy having one sense so keenly attuned.'

'Yeah, yeah. Save your sob story for your Super Friends at the Justice League.'

* * *

Lance and I were doing yard work one afternoon when Phillip stopped by.

I was on the roof.

Phillip got out of his car, shaded his eyes with his hand and said, 'Rachel?'

I said, 'What are you doing here?'

'Mother's birthday. What are you doing up there?'

'I'm sweeping the bastard roof clear of a year's worth of rotting pine straw is what I'm doing. Lance won't take his little girl pink panties off and get his ass up here to do it. So here I am.'

'Who?'

I pointed to the back gate where Lance was standing with his hands in his pockets. He said, 'Lance. That would be me.'

Phillip waved.

Lance nodded.

Phillip said, 'Can't you just hire somebody to do that?'

I said, 'Don't talk to me.'

'Hold on. I'm coming up.' He exchanged a few 'nice weather we're having' pleasantries with Lance and then climbed up the ladder. 'Damn. How long have you been up here? Sit down for a minute. You're going to have a stroke. Your face is blood red.'

'I'm not hot. I'm mad.'

'Calm down. It's nothing to be mad about.'

'No? It isn't? Well how about this? I'm fucking sick of being the only one around here that does anything. He could stay up all night playing video games but he can't get his ass up here on the roof.'

Lance said, 'I have acrophobia.'

'Oh grow a pair, for fuck's sake.'

Lance was standing by the ladder with his arms crossed. He was staring at us.

I was furious.

I threw the broom at him and screamed, 'Quit staring up here you fucking pussy!'

Phillip said, 'No. No. Don't say that. She's sorry Vance.'

I said, 'No I'm not.'

Lance said, 'My name is Lance. Not Vance.'

'Perhaps it would be best, Lance, if you went in the house while Rachel and I finished up here.'

★ ★ ★

Our relationship was without passion, but Lance wasn't

incapable of strong emotions.

He fell madly in love with a live-action role player in New Zealand. They met on the internet. Her screen name was Evema Dala, friend of the Elves. Her real name was Carol Newton.

The last I heard of either of them, Evema was nurturing the psychic abilities her parents stifled when she was a child and she and Lance were marketing a pilot to television network executives about a married couple of forensic investigators. One psychic, the other straight.

Texas is a pretty big place.

We hadn't been driving as long as I would have liked when Noah called.

'I'm exhausted. Not enough sleep last night. You mind if we stop in Sweetwater?'

I said, 'You stop. I'm not.'

'Never mind, I'll be ok. I guess. Hey, keep an eye out back here won't you? If my vehicle should leave the road call…'

'Fine.'

Sweetwater it was.

★ ★ ★

As we neared the Sweetwater exit Noah passed me.

He motioned for me to follow him off the interstate.

I thought about going on without him but knew there was no point.

He drove straight to the Longhorn Motel's parking lot.

The place wasn't much to look at.

Noah got out of the Navigator and said, 'Sweetwater's finest.'

I said, 'Are you sure you want to stay here?'

'I don't know why not. According to the sign there it's: "no bugs, no drugs, no thugs". Hopefully they'll make an exception for you.'

'Very funny.'

'Who could ask for more? Or less? Which would it be?'

Phillip called while I was getting my bags out of the trunk. He said, 'Hey Babysnake.'

'Hello you. How's things?'

'Fine. How's things witchoo?'

'Yah, fine.'

'Will you be home for Christmas?'

'Where's home?'

'Save the drama for your mama. Spend Christmas with me.'

I was quiet.

'Silence. Nothing but crickets. Is that a yes or a no?'

'Phillip, if anything should ever happen to me, I want you to know how much you mean to me.'

'What's going to happen to you?'

'Nothing. I just wanted to say it. We should live each day like it's our last. Shouldn't we?'

'Who is this? Hello? Why have you got Rachel's phone?'

'Forget it.'

'God. Have you been watching Oprah again?'

'I was serious.'

'I know you were. I don't like it.'

'I don't feel good, Phillip. I'm sad.'

'Well, let's do something about it but as it stands, it's like you're trying to hold *me* hostage with *your* life and that's no good. Tell me where you are.'

'I'm in Sweetwater with Noah.'

'Please tell me you're not married again.'

'I'm not married again.'

'Swear to me you aren't going to do anything stupid. I can't stand it, Rachel.'

'I swear.'

'That includes marrying this Noah person.'

'Don't worry, he's not my type.'

'None of them have been your type. That's what worries.'

★ ★ ★

By that time, I was in the habit of carrying the cherry-coloured box with me wherever I went.

I met Noah inside the hotel restaurant. I put the cherry-coloured box in the middle of the table between us.

Noah asked, 'Who was that?'

'Phillip.'

'Sounded like a heated discussion.'

'I'm not made for this world. I just want everything to stop.'

'Let's get you home.'

'What is it today with people and me "going home"? You fucking go home. If you had any fucking pride you'd have a real job, not babysitting the boss's daughter.'

'You're a little hellcat, aren't you. Can you actually hear yourself when you say things like that?'

'Yes, I can. Yes, I know.'

'Well, stop it.'

'One more spoon and I will.'

'You're depressed. You need professional help. You've been through a traumatic time.'

'All I've been through is *life*. Everybody tells me what I am. Everybody knows me better than I know myself. Everybody knows what's best for me. Sick of it.'

'Let's think about that for a minute. You are out here in the middle of nowhere, collecting spoons and planning to kill yourself.'

'I am not.'

Noah tapped on the cherry-coloured box and said, 'Yes, you are. I read your Things to Do List.'

★ ★ ★

We spent the night in Sweetwater.

Noah wouldn't let me have a room of my own.

I told him not to worry, that I couldn't kill myself until I had the last spoon. That didn't seem to matter.

We ate at a barbecue place called The Tasty Pig.

We were seated, picnic style on a long bench with several other couples.

I decided to have catfish. I thought Noah was going to have

a seizure.

'Catfish! I can't believe you'd come to a famous BBQ joint and have catfish.'

'Catfish is delicious.'

'Yeah, if you like to eat mud.'

'I don't expect you to know anything about good food being from the northwest. It's just good times and moose on a stick up there.'

Noah said, 'Try the frisky brisket.'

'I don't want the frisky brisket.'

The waitress said, 'The catfish is real good.'

Noah said, 'Ok then. I'll have the brisket and we'll start off with some BBQ ribs.'

There wasn't a single napkin in the whole place. When the ribs arrived I asked for some napkins and the waitress laughed. She said, 'Honey, you're supposed to just go ahead and wipe yourself off on the bread.'

Something about that seemed profoundly wrong. I took to it immediately.

There was a sign hanging over the door: 2 tons sold weekly. I asked the waitress if that was true.

She said, 'Nah. That sign's been up there forever. More like three tons or so a week now.'

★ ★ ★

I took a shower later that night.

When I came out of the bathroom Noah was on the phone. He finished the call quickly.

I asked him who it was. He said it was Gloria.

I asked, 'Do you smell blueberry muffins?'

'I don't think so.'

I walked around the room, smelling. 'Sometimes I swear that I can smell blueberry muffins. That or cigarette smoke. But I can't ever track it down. It's usually late at night.'

'Maybe you actually do smell them.'

'Maybe so.'

'Are you feeling better? It seems like you're feeling better.'

'I never feel better. Especially when somebody asks me if I'm feeling better.'

Scorecard: Four.

October 8, 2004: Connor McMann.

When I think of my fourth wedding, I think: Pocatello, Idaho.

I've only been to Pocatello once.

It was enough.

News of our engagement didn't go over well with Connor's parents. His mother was grief-stricken because her son was marrying a woman she'd never met. In order to stave off a full-blown nervous breakdown and the disintegration of civilization as we knew it, Mohammed agreed to go to the mountain.

That's how I ended up a blushing, bridling bride in Pocatello.

Connor's mother, Rosemary, insisted on handling all of the arrangements. The only time I spoke directly to her about the wedding she called and asked, 'Do you like the Bee Gees for reception music?'

I said, 'I'm not much of a Bee Gees fan to be honest.'

'Is my son there?'

I handed the phone to Connor and the first thing I heard him say was: 'Yeah, I love the Bee Gees.'

I became concerned while we were waiting for our luggage at the airport when Connor told me that his mother hadn't been out of the house in six years.

I said, 'You mean she's just a homebody?'

'Definitely. And literally though, she hasn't left the house in six years or seven years, something like that.'

'Why not?'

'She's amaxophobic.'

'Humour me why don't you? Could you just tell me what the hell an amaxophobic is?'

'It's not catching or anything for God's sake. The woman's just afraid to ride in cars.'

'That doesn't mean she can't go out of the house.'

'She doesn't like to walk either.'

'I guess she's not picking us up at the airport then, is she?'

'That's not funny. It's a real clinical phobia, you know.'

'Why would she insist on handling all the arrangements for the wedding if she doesn't ever leave the house? What's she doing for food at the reception?'

'She said something about ordering pizza afterwards.'

Connor's father was late to pick us up. We were just about to get a taxi when he drove up. He looked worried.

He said, 'Rachel? You must be Rachel. I'm Lonnie.'

'It's nice to meet you Lonnie.'

He hugged Connor and said, 'Listen, your mother isn't well. She's really been overwhelmed by the responsibility of planning this whole wedding all by herself and what with all this anxiety, she's broken out something terrible with the shingles. She won't let anybody in the house.'

Connor said, 'She'll be fine. Let's go home and I'll talk some sense into her.'

But Rosemary wasn't fine. She stuck to her guns. She wouldn't let a single soul in the house. I ended up changing into my dress in the garage and we got married on the driveway with twenty of Connor's friends from grammar and high school. Some, he hadn't seen in thirty years.

Before we left his mother opened a window and called me over. I had to step into the flowerbed to get close enough to hear her.

She said, 'I hope you aren't marrying my son for his money.'

I said, 'I didn't know he had any.'

'Here.' She handed me coupons for pizza delivery. 'Enjoy.'

We spent our honeymoon watching CNN and eating ice cream in a hotel room in Chubbuck.

★ ★ ★

When Bailiff Eddie Walker said that my fourth husband didn't look like he could screw his way out of a wet paper bag, he was wrong. In fact, that's about all Connor could do well.

Our first Valentine's Day together we ate the obligatory romantic dinner, opened the obligatory gifts of chocolate and crotchless panties, read the obligatory sentimental greeting cards (Hallmark has a lot to answer for as regards the condition of 'modern' man) but then the conversation took a twist. We were visited by the ghosts of love past. Some women are threatened by past lovers. Not me. I tend to be more concerned about current ones.

Connor asked, 'How many people have you slept with?'

A couple of numbers popped into my head. I thought for a moment and realized that, although I hadn't slept with *that* many people, it was at least enough to require a bit of thought, perhaps pen and paper, even a calculator – but that's still no indication of a vast number. I'm no good at math and to get to this number, I was pretty sure I'd run out of fingers and toes.

While I was thinking Connor said, 'I've slept with three hundred and twenty-seven.'

'Three hundred and twenty-seven what?'

'Women, silly.'

'What number am I?'

'Are you sure you want to know?'

'If I am less than three hundred and twenty-seven, probably not.'

'Nah, babe. That's you.'

I considered the sheer effort involved in sleeping with that many women and then I considered the actual volume of material produced during orgasm, if indeed orgasm was reached each time. I shuddered.

'Hang on a second, I'll show you something.'

While he was gone I considered what implications this had for me and another trip back to the free clinic. I shuddered again.

Connor went into the bedroom. I was a bit anxious about what evidence he might produce but he came back with a tatty black notebook with a picture of a Tonka truck on the cover.

It contained names and dates and details for all three hundred and twenty-seven encounters. For a moment all the fucking was beside the point. I was amazed by his meticulous clerical skills. Some entries were even accompanied by illustrations drawn well enough to leave no graphic detail to the imagination. I found myself nodding with approval to the entries involving multiple partners because it seemed to answer the concern of exactly how *does* one manage to sleep with *that* many women.

As he flipped through the pages making the occasional comment, I stopped him at one particularly busy time. He said, 'Yeah, I was married to a girl called Evelyn then.'

'I didn't know you were married before.'

'Yeah.'

'Why didn't you tell me?'

'Dunno. Didn't occur to me and you didn't ask, I guess. But you've been married before so what does it matter?'

'I'm not saying it does matter. Just curious.'

'Evelyn was young. Just a girl really. I called her Evy. But she was ok as far as girls go. Pretty, doe-eyed blonde. Her mom was real old-fashioned though and Evy had picked up stuff from her. Sex was sort of old-fashioned with her, top on, lights off, missionary only, you know. And she had real clear ideas about keeping a house and stuff like that. She liked to invite friends over for charades or canasta or croquet in the yard. Fuck me, I didn't even know what canasta was! But she'd make finger food and I'd get beer and stuff and they weren't bad. But Evy was famous for drinking too many peach wine coolers. I mean she flat out loved the stuff. She'd get tanked, reveal something horribly personal about her childhood and then nod off to sleep on the couch. I didn't mind. Three of the best sexual experiences of my life happened while Evy was asleep. Here, let me see the book and I'll show you.'

Number 87: Kathy – husband skipped fondue night, bowling instead. Don't blame him. Kathy: braced against front quarter panel of new riding lawn mower, told me to come over and see about her little grassy patch.

Number 88: Andrea Chambers – Sunday School class with Evy. Baked real good German chocolate cake. Fucked her from behind, bent over the kitchen table. Could see tits bouncing in oven door reflection.

Number 89: Marcy. Andrea Chambers' little sister. Could suck the chrome off a bumper. Head in the laundry room.

'Thing was Andrea and Marcy compared notes and then told Evy. Well, she up and back home to Lipton, North Carolina with her parents. I didn't hear anything from her for seven months. See here, that's this next real busy time.' He pointed to the next couple of pages in his 'sexual log'.

'I see that.'

'Anyway, I had a lawyer draw up divorce papers, standard stuff, and I went to Lipton to get her to sign. Her father shot the side mirror off my Buick. Her brother, Larry, eventually came out of the house and found me behind the woodpile where I landed when gunfire broke out. He beat me damned near senseless with a piece of firewood. I woke up. It was dark and there was a basset hound sleeping next to me.

'I didn't hear nothing from Evy for three years, not until I came home from work to find Larry watching television in my den. I got myself a beer out of the fridge and asked him if he could use one.'

'He said, "Sign those papers on the dining-room table. Evy wants out".'

'He told me that she was engaged to be married to Stephen Driver, some guy she'd known from high school who'd opened a business digging septic tanks and field lines. Before he left he told me not to try and win her back or to go getting any ideas.'

I looked at him, tried to smile and said, 'Ideas are dangerous things.'

What comes around goes around.

I wish I could say that it was just an experiment between two curious youths. But I can't.

I was twenty-eight when I had sex with my cousin. I am compelled to further clarify that this was a 'second' cousin. Although it was years ago, I am still reluctant to name names so, for the purposes of this confession, I shall use a pseudonym: Bird. Bird comes to mind because his legs were quite skinny, his neck quite long and at one point I became disoriented and felt as though I was being wrestled to the ground by an ostrich.

The experience was no rite of passage. There was no tender deflowering. I can't even say that it was a drunken, impassioned mistake. Don't misunderstand me, we were plenty drunk but in retrospect it seems that intoxication was a sort of mollifying foreplay.

Afterwards, I asked Bird if he enjoyed it.

He paused for a moment, pursed his lips and looked into space as if he were trying to read the answer from a distant billboard. He said, 'It was a lot like having sex with my sister.' I didn't have the guts to ask him if the comparison was literal or metaphorical.

In over my head.

My father kidnapped me when I was sixteen.

I was in my bedroom performing surgery on a pair of faded Levis with a razor blade. I was into sliced and frayed at the time.

There was a knock at the door.

I turned down the music and said, 'Who is it?' I couldn't make out what they were saying. 'I can't *hear* you. Who is it?'

The door opened just a crack and my father whispered, 'Are you decent?'

'That's a loaded question.'

'Can I come in?'

'Yes, why are you whispering?'

He closed the door and said, 'Is your mother here?'

I said, 'No, she's having her eyebrows bleached.'

'What about Julie?'

'She's at the movies. Why?'

'Do you want to go to Paris?'

'When?'

'Now.'

'What about Thanksgiving?'

'What about it?'

'It's tomorrow.'

'Really?'

'Really.'

'I could get you tickets to the Dire Straits for tomorrow. They're playing at the Palais Omnisports de Bercy.'

'Give me a while to pack.'

'No time. I'll buy you new things once we get there.'

I was in my father's private jet and somewhere over the Atlantic before it I was able to process the fact that I was going to France.

Comme c'est intéressant!

★ ★ ★

When he called Mother to tell her where we were I don't think she'd realized I was gone.

After she had time to get properly mad, the story changed.

She told a harrowing tale of a mother's grief: not being able to find her daughter. She said she looked all over the house and hours later when I hadn't come home she called the police, the hospitals, the morgues and even had me paged at the grocery store.

We never outlived the shame of leaving her and Julie alone for Thanksgiving.

Julie later said it was the most maudlin day of her life.

Apparently Mother threw all the food she'd bought in the garbage and Julie ended up eating celery and peanut butter.

★ ★ ★

My father made good on his promise.

He set me free on the streets of Paris armed with cash, platinum credit cards, Dire Straits tickets and a chaperone named Chance.

I thought I had seen beauty.

I thought I had experienced pleasure.

But that day was truly one of the best (and worst) of my entire life.

Paris was ok.

Chance was transformative.

He was much older. When I say much, I mean: much. I was sixteen. Chance was thirty-two. There wasn't anything dramatically handsome about him. He wasn't a model in the rough. But he was rough around the edges and charming and I could tell the moment I saw him that he was a bit dangerous in a well packaged, well respected kind of way.

Chance was the son of one of my father's business partners. He agreed to 'babysit' me for the day while my father hosted some international gala.

He toyed with me for a while the way a fat cat toys with a little mouse trapped in a corner. I flirted with him mercilessly. It didn't take long for the tension to amp well beyond control and at one point he scooped me up in his arms and pushed me against a wall in a very dirty alley.

He said, 'Enfant naïf, pourquoi tu me provoques ainsi?'

I said, 'Je ne suis pas un enfant. Laisse-moi te montrer.'

'You are the boss's baby daughter.'

'Is *that* what he told you.'

'Oui, you say different?'

I don't know where I learned to be a vixen but that day the little tramp showed her face, really for the first time. I'd never had a chance to be much of a vixen with Jack. Even though we'd kissed and had a few awkward fumbling sessions we'd certainly never had sex. But that afternoon I moved Chance's hand down between my legs and said, 'I say different. Oui.'

My father was asleep on the couch when I got back to the hotel that night. He woke up long enough to tell me that I looked flushed. He felt my forehead to see if I had a fever. He said, 'I ordered an extra club sandwich for you in case you were hungry, darling.'

I said, Thanks Daddy.'

I took it to my room and cried.

★ ★ ★

Mother was distracted when we got home.

She was screaming on the phone to a customer service representative. She said, 'I can't understand you. I can't understand a word you're saying. I want to speak with somebody in America!'

Julie was watching television. She muted the volume and took the phone away from Mother. She said, 'Hello? This is Missus Bennett's daughter. Yes... Yes... Yes... I can understand you. Let me see if I can translate for my mother.'

Mother said, 'I wanted to talk to an American.'

'He understood that part, Mother. Could you please just tell me what you want so I can get this straightened out for you and finish watching my show.'

Mother turned to look at us standing in the hall holding our luggage. She said, 'Oh, they're back.'

Julie said, 'Yes, I see that. What is your account password?'

'Clark Gable.'

I never promised you the world.

Emma forgave me for the fork incident.

When she called I didn't recognize her voice.

I was in a crowded buffet-style restaurant and there were seven unenthusiastic waitresses singing and clapping happy birthday to a man wearing the birthday sombrero.

Emma said, 'I think it's time we got this whole thing out in the open.'

'I don't know what to say other than I'm sorry and I'll try not to stab you again.'

'There's more to it than that.'

'Enlighten me.'

Emma said, 'I'm trying to turn my life around. I've stopped drinking.'

'Good for you.'

'Yeah. I joined this Christian alcohol support group and I feel like I've really got a handle on things now. Strictly special occasions from now on.'

'You still drink on special occasions?'

'Yes, only special occasions.'

'I hate to point out the obvious but technically that negates the statement "I've stopped drinking".'

'Even Jesus drank wine in moderation.'

'I don't think he was buying boxed wine on a two for one special at the supermarket.'

Emma said, 'Would you please try to hold your negative energy in check. I'm trying to heal myself and mend relationships through the power of Jesus Christ and I don't need your pessimistic double talk.'

'Ok.'

'Listen, what I'm trying to say is that there are certain

glorious truths that need to come to light before I can continue down the path of recovery.'

I said, 'I'm not sure I've got the stomach for glorious truth.'

'Rachel, here it is: I am in a committed, loving relationship with Daniel.'

'Daniel who?'

'Your old Daniel.'

I couldn't think of anything to say. I was sitting in a noisy restaurant watching my soft-serve ice cream melt over the edges of a speckled plastic bowl. The kid in the booth behind me needed his diaper changed and his brother needed his ass spanked for throwing spaghetti on the floor. The table of ladies next to me was laughing loudly and stuffing their big open-mouthed loud laughing faces with macaroni and mashed potatoes and cheesy cauliflower bake. And for all that, I still couldn't shake the image of Daniel asking me to clip his toenails.

Emma said, 'Are you there?'

'Yes.'

'I know this must be difficult for you. Imagining one of your discarded lovers in a caring relationship with your best friend, but try to keep things in a healthy perspective. After all, you left him.'

'That's enough glorious truth for one day, thank you very much. May I make a final suggestion in the spirit of Christian love and compassion?'

'Yes.'

'Get yourself some strong antibiotics.'

The final stretch.

I knew the whole Sweetwater stop was a ruse when I saw Gloria at breakfast.

Noah *insisted* that we have something to eat even though I *insisted* that I wasn't hungry.

I was still stuffed full of cholesterol, saturated fat and catfish from the night before at The Tasty Pig.

Noah said, 'Let's sit in here.' He pulled back a folding, plastic divider between the main restaurant and a larger seating area.

I said, 'I don't think that part is open yet.'

'It's ok. Come on in.'

And there she was. Gloria was seated alone. The rest of the place was empty. The table was clad in a crisp white tablecloth and laid out before her was a silver serving set. Granola. Mandarin Oranges. Grapes. Milk. Tea.

She said, 'Leave us, Noah.'

I sat down and said, 'You look like a mob boss sitting in here alone with this spread.'

She said, 'I like that image. It works for me. Here, try some of this granola. I get it from a place in Wisconsin. It's all organic.'

'I suppose it's pointless to ask you what you're doing out here in the middle of nowhere.'

'Isn't it what you wanted? Somebody to come riding in on a white horse to save you? To insist that you stop being foolish and forget about this ridiculous spoon suicide scheme?'

'Where's my father?'

'You really should try some of the oranges with the granola. Your father is spending Christmas in Munich with Miles. Apparently they've had quite a run-in with one of the more inexperienced members of staff. Your father set his fancy on one of the antiques in the Mandarin Suite and suggested to the concierge that he wanted to purchase it. It didn't go well. Now I do believe he'll have the whole Mandarin Hotel in his back pocket.'

'And Mother? What she got to say about him spending Christmas away?'

Gloria pushed the bowl of grapes closer to me. She said, 'She's checked herself into a retreat just outside of Salt Lake City. She's suffering from exhaustion.'

'Exhaustion from what?'

'Life is all a bit much for her right now, it seems. The family is falling apart, so she says.'

'Has the family ever been *together*?'

Gloria said, 'While I was getting your mother checked in, Julie called hysterical. She said that if you and your mother could run away to rehab for no good reason, she could too. So I had to make arrangements for her to come to Salt Lake City too. She says she's staying there until the baby is born. Frank has been banned from the premises. And then there's you...'

'What about me?'

'Don't make me laugh. You are the most worrisome of all. You're out here in the middle of the desert collecting spoons and planning to off yourself. I mean if it wasn't so truly pitiful it would be laughable.'

'It's funny. Yes.'

'I'm not minimizing your feelings but surely you see how ludicrous the whole thing is? Certainly you don't think we're going to allow it. Do you?'

I said, 'I think I just chipped a tooth on this granola.'

'It's better if you let it sit in milk for a moment.'

'I appreciate this Gloria. You've been good to me and whether you think it is pitiful or laughable one thing is true, I do love you.'

'I love you too, kiddo.'

★ ★ ★

My cell phone was ringing as I left the hotel.

It was Phillip calling.

I didn't answer.

Noah said, 'He'll be worried.'

I tried four places before I finally found a New Mexico state spoon in a roadside tourist trap in Eunice, New Mexico.

I thought it would be a nice gesture to buy Christmas gifts and have Noah take them back, sort of a last goodwill gesture on my part. I bought Mother a set of salt and pepper shakers made in the likeness of two amorous cacti. I bought my father a license plate keychain which read: DAD. I bought Julie a box of chocolate-covered jalapeños.

I also bought a used Buck knife. I hid it in my pocket and was determined that if they wouldn't let me go gracefully, I would go in a hail of tears and arterial spray.

When I came out of the store I made direct eye contact with Gloria.

Gloria was in my car.

My car was rolling backwards.

When she saw me she wheeled the car around quickly and even laid a little rubber as she was pulling out onto the busy two-lane road. I ran through a cloud of dust, screaming for her to stop. When I got to the edge of the parking lot, in complete frustration, I let out one long scream and threw my cherry-coloured box, completed set of 50 State Spoons and all, at the car as it sped away.

The box splintered. A blue Dodge Ram pick-up truck ran over it. Spoons scattered across the pavement.

Noah was standing by the Navigator with the passenger door open. He was waiting for me to get in.

I screamed from the road, 'Did you know about this?'

He said, 'Come on, Rachel, get in. Let's go home.'

'Did you know they were going to do this?'

He started walking toward me. 'What did you think?

Seriously. Did you really think that we were going to let you collect these stupid spoons and then kill yourself in a dingy hotel?'

I turned my back to him and started walking.

'Rachel! Wait. Here, speak to your father first. I'm dialling.'

I didn't stop.

'I'm dialling, Rachel. Stop right there.'

★ ★ ★

It occurred to me that most American life consists of driving somewhere and then returning home, wondering why the hell you went out.

I wasn't going home. I didn't even know where home was.

As I walked along the desert highway, Christmas gifts in one hand, melting chocolate jalapeños in the other, I thought: it's not too late. I could still kill myself. I don't need the spoons.

But for some reason I did need them. They were part of it.

The plan was: collect all the spoons and then kill myself.

The spoons were gone. I didn't have a new plan.

I looked back.

Noah was driving slowly at a safe distance behind me. Traffic was backed up for as far as I could see. Semi-trucks and cars were blowing their horns furiously, passing when they could and dousing me with hot air from their hot engines. Some of them screamed at me. A couple of them whistled. One woman threw an empty beer bottle.

It was a lot of fuss for not so much.

★ ★ ★

One time, when I was little, I hid in a cardboard box in the garage and waited for my father to come home from work.

I waited all day.

I waited all night.

Nobody looked for me.

He didn't come home.

Early the next morning I heard footsteps. When they passed by the box I reached out and grabbed ankles.

It was Minnie.

She screamed and kicked me.

That's how I lost my two front teeth.

When she realized what she'd done, she cried. She got down on the cold concrete floor with me and pulled me up on her lap. She used her shirt to wipe blood from my mouth.

Minnie said, 'Oh baby. Baby. I'm so, so sorry. Promise me you'll never do that again. Promise me.' She held my head back and looked at my swollen lips. She was still crying. She said, 'What were you doing in there?'

I said, 'I wanted to surprise Daddy when he got home.'

She said, 'Rachel, your daddy is upstairs.'

★ ★ ★

I didn't last long.

Some time just after my heels began to blister and just before the chocolate-covered jalapeños turned to soup and dripped out the bottom of the box, I stopped.

And right there in the desert, I gave up.

I didn't say anything.

I didn't do anything.

I just stood there.

The world continued around me and I was acutely aware of every sound, the feel of every single inch of my skin pressed against an opposing force which I suppose was all the unseen things we take for granted or don't believe in because we can't see them with the naked eye or buy them on Amazon. The pain from my blistered feet radiated through my body, rising to meet the longing I felt for Jack; it moved slowly until it reached that place where I kept all the love and pain I felt for him.

It was only then that I realized something. It was my head that felt like it was going to split open and leave me dry and lifeless. My pain for Jack was in my head, not my heart.

I put my hand to my heart and acknowledged what I'd been ignoring all these years.

Noah had stopped the Navigator and got out. He was standing beside me quietly.

I looked at him and said, 'It isn't Jack.'

'No?'

'No. I don't think it ever was.'

'Does the other one know?'

'Can I borrow your cell phone?'

He said, 'Sure.'

I dialled the number. I got voicemail.

I handed Noah the phone back and asked, 'Where's the nearest airport?'

When we got back to the Navigator his phone rang. He answered it.

'Hello. Noah Kwiatkowski. Yes. Who is calling? Hold on a minute.' Noah handed me the phone and said, 'He didn't recognize the number is why he didn't answer.'

I said, 'I'm going to catch a flight from Lubbock, Texas. Will you pick me up from the airport?'

I handed Noah his phone back.

Noah asked, 'Why does he call you Babysnake?'

I said, 'I've no idea.'

'It suits you.'

Acknowledgements

Michael Schmidt, Adrian Searle, Charlie Taylor, Nicola Taylor, Iain Maloney, Jon Barnes, Amy Elias, Alison Chapman, Remona Hopper, Mindy Ryan, Katie Baasen, Leslie Holland, Marshall Alexander, Tara Alexander.

Mom, Dad, Debbie, Brian, Brandon, John, Alex.

Just a few of the people I wish to thank for helping make this novel possible.